A Dead Bore

ANOTHER JOHN PICKETT MYSTERY

A Dead Bore

SHERI COBB SOUTH

FIVE STAR
A part of Gale, Cengage Learning

Detroit • New York • San Francisco • New Haven, Conn • Waterville, Maine • London

Five Star Publishing, a part of Gale, Cengage Learning.

Set in 11 pt. Plantin.

Printed on permanent paper.

LIBRARY OF CONGRESS CATALOGING-IN-PUBLICATION DATA

South, Sheri Cobb.
A dead bore : another John Pickett mystery / Sheri Cobb South. — 1st ed.
p. cm.
ISBN-13: 978-1-59414-711-1 (hardcover : alk. paper)
ISBN-10: 1-59414-711-6 (hardcover : alk. paper)
1. Police—London—England—Fiction. 2. Aristocracy (Social class)—Fiction. 3. Widows—Fiction. 4. Yorkshire (England)—Fiction. I. Title.
PS3569.O755D43 2008
813′.54—dc22 2008037872

First Edition. First Printing: December 2008.
Published in 2008 in conjunction with Tekno Books and Ed Gorman.

Printed in the United States of America
1 2 3 4 5 6 7 12 11 10 09 08

To the Cobb women: Aggie, Jayne, Pam, April, and Kelli.
Long may they reign.

Prologue

In Which Lady Fieldhurst Ponders an Invitation

The weather on this June morning was particularly fine, but no ray of sunlight illuminated the Berkeley Square drawing room where two ladies sat drinking tea. The gold velvet draperies adorning the windows of this elegantly appointed chamber were tightly closed, for this was a house of mourning. Grief, however, was not the emotion uppermost in the mind of at least one of the pair, a dashing brunette dressed in vibrant shades of blue.

"Yorkshire?" exclaimed the Countess of Dunnington in tones of deepest revulsion, returning her teacup to its saucer with a disapproving *clink.* "You would go to Yorkshire in July? My dear Julia, you must be mad!"

Lady Fieldhurst, sipping her tea, smiled at her friend's vehemence. The younger of the two ladies by some ten years, she was clad in the sober black of the recent widow, and was as fair as the fashionable Lady Dunnington was dark. "Mad? Nonsense, Emily! Why do you say so?"

"No one goes to Yorkshire unless they are escaping from something—a dunning tradesman, perhaps, or an importunate lover."

"Or a thoroughly unpleasant scandal," added Lady Fieldhurst.

"A scandal which was none of your making," Emily reminded her. "Still, if you wish to leave London for a time, you would do better to come with me to Brighton. At least you should find plenty there to amuse you."

Lady Fieldhurst, refilling the cups from a silver teapot, arched a skeptical eyebrow. "Indeed, I should—far more amusement than is seemly for a widow of less than two months' standing."

"And you so fond of poor Fieldhurst, too," sighed Lady Dunnington, shaking her head with mock sorrow.

The widowed viscountess gave her friend a reproachful look, but held her ground. In truth, her reluctance to accompany Lady Dunnington to Brighton had less to do with her recent bereavement than with her desire to avoid the company of certain gentlemen of her acquaintance, the first and foremost of these being Emily's latest paramour. She frequently wondered what her friend saw in a foppish and by all accounts penniless young man several years her junior. At six-and-twenty, however, Lady Fieldhurst was too much a woman of the world to be shocked by the connection. Indeed, she had been on the verge of taking a lover of her own when fate had intervened in the form of Viscount Fieldhurst's untimely demise.

"Lord Rupert will be in Brighton," observed Lady Dunnington, regarding her with a measuring look.

Lady Fieldhurst colored slightly at having her thoughts so accurately read. "You have quite decided me, Emily! If Lord Rupert is to be in Brighton, I must certainly go to Yorkshire. Between the pair of us, Rupert and I have given the tabbies quite enough to gossip about already."

Lady Dunnington was not deceived. "Aha! Then I was right when I suggested you might be escaping an importunate lover. Are Lord Rupert's hopes to be dashed, then?"

"I don't know," confessed Lady Fieldhurst, sipping her tea and wishing it was not too early in the day for sherry. "I haven't yet decided. I only want to go away for awhile so that I may be left alone. If I am fortunate, no one else at this house party will have ever heard of me, much less my recent notoriety."

"My dear Julia, I fear you are doomed to disappointment.

Society circles are not so large as to allow anonymity. Depend upon it, everyone knows of your narrow escape from the gallows, even those whom you have never met."

"Do you think so?" asked Lady Fieldhurst, crestfallen. "I am scarcely acquainted with the hostess, but my recollections of Lady Anne Hollingshead are that she is excruciatingly proper. I cannot imagine why she should have invited a guest so recently featured in all the scandal sheets. I know nothing of the rest of the family. I have never met her husband, for instance—"

"Nor are likely to, so long as you are fixed in London," Emily put in. "I believe Sir Gerald prefers the country life."

"He seems an odd match for Lady Anne, then," observed Lady Fieldhurst. "She has always seemed to me the very personification of the Society matron. During my come-out, I lived in fear of a disapproving glance through her lorgnette. I should have thought her husband would be one of Society's leading lights—a member of Parliament, perhaps, or a diplomat."

Lady Dunnington helped herself to a slice of seed cake and leaned forward with a confidential air. "Ah, but Sir Gerald was not her first choice. In her mad youth—if one can imagine Lady Anne ever having had such a thing—she was set to make a brilliant match."

"What happened?"

Emily shrugged. "He died. I don't recall the details. It all happened before my time. She is several years older than I, you know."

"Everyone is older than you, darling, including your eldest son," retorted Lady Fieldhurst without malice. "Still, it is a sad story, but at least she found a second chance at happiness."

"And so shall you, my dear—but not if you insist on burying yourself in Yorkshire." As Lady Fieldhurst opened her mouth to protest, Lady Dunnington raised a silencing hand. "Very well, I shan't tease you on the subject. Go to Yorkshire if you feel you must, but I predict you will be bored to tears within a se'ennight!"

Chapter 1
In Which Are Introduced the Local Gentry

The light was beginning to fade by the time the hired post-chaise lurched to a halt before the imposing stone façade of Hollingshead Place. Lady Fieldhurst regarded the stark gray edifice through the rain-streaked carriage windows and wondered, not for the first time, why she had been so determined to come. Three days and two hundred miles ago, when she had first set out from London, Emily's predictions of unmitigated boredom had been easily dismissed. After all, Emily had never been rumored to have murdered her husband, and so had no notion of how very welcome the prospect of boredom could seem. In the end, the matter had been decided by a letter from the dowager Lady Fieldhurst, who insisted that Julia spend the first few months of her widowhood quietly at the Dower House in the company of her mama-in-law. Although imminently suitable, at least in the eyes of Society, this prospect was so daunting that Lady Fieldhurst had penned her acceptance to Lady Anne Hollingshead that very day.

A liveried footman rushed out of the house to meet her with an unfurled umbrella, and Lady Fieldhurst steeled herself with the reflection that, no matter how dreary her present prospects, her situation might have been much worse: she might have been obliged to spend a rainy day trapped inside the Dower House with her mother-in-law. Fortified with this knowledge, she turned up the collar of her black kerseymere pelisse, disembarked from the vehicle, and accepted the footman's protective escort to the house.

She was pleased—and to no small degree relieved—to discover that its somber exterior was deceptive. Inside, a cheerful fire burned merrily on a massive hearth, reflecting on the black-and-white marble tiles of the floor and turning the richly carved wainscoting to burnished gold. Framed portraits of earlier generations of Hollingsheads gazed down at the newcomer from their heavy gilt frames, and twin suits of armor flanked the staircase, but even these daunting entities seemed well pleased to welcome a viscountess to Hollingshead Place. A movement overhead drew her eye upward to the tall, graceful lady descending the curved staircase.

"My dear Lady Fieldhurst," exclaimed Lady Anne Hollingshead, her arms outstretched in greeting. "Such dismal weather with which to welcome you! I do hope the roads were not too badly rutted?"

"Not at all," murmured Lady Fieldhurst with more courtesy than accuracy. Lady Anne's elegance made her painfully aware of her rain-spattered and travel-stained appearance. To her chagrin, she felt more like the gauche debutante she had once been than the modish and slightly scandalous Society matron she had become.

"Shocking amount of rain we've had lately, absolutely shocking!" put in Sir Gerald Hollingshead, shaking his grizzled head as he lumbered down the stairs in his wife's wake.

Observing his descent, Lady Fieldhurst found her earlier speculations confirmed: he did indeed seem an odd match for Lady Anne. He was fully two decades his wife's senior, but this in itself was unremarkable; fifteen years had separated the late Lord Fieldhurst from his bride, and Lady Fieldhurst knew of many matches where the age difference was a quarter century or more. No, the difference had less to do with the ages of the parties involved than with their respective appearances. Unlike the stylish Lady Anne, Sir Gerald was dressed for comfort rather than fashion in a loose-fitting tail coat, buckskin breeches, and cuffed top-boots. Lady Fieldhurst received the impression that he would be far more content to be outdoors with a gun over his shoulder and hounds at his heels. Lady Fieldhurst, herself country-bred, was reminded of her own doting papa, and found herself liking her host on sight. Still, she could not but acknowledge that he and Lady Anne made an ill-assorted pair.

"Pray accept my condolences on the loss of your husband," Lady Anne continued in a more serious vein. "How dreadful for you, to be widowed at such a young age, and in *such* a fashion!"

Privately, Lady Fieldhurst considered being left a widow at the age of six-and-twenty far less dreadful than coming within Ames-ace of hanging for murder. But in the past two months she had perfected the art of mouthing platitudes, and it was this habit to which she now sought recourse. "You are too kind, my lady. My husband's death came as a great shock, but I take comfort in the knowledge that his sufferings were brief."

"Such sentiments do you credit, my dear," said Lady Anne, squeezing Julia's hands warmly. "I hope that while you are with us, you will be able to forget your recent loss, at least for a little while. I fear one or two of our guests have been obliged to send their regrets on account of the weather, but I have contrived to throw together a modest dinner party to introduce you to the local gentry. But I must not keep you standing here in those wet clothes! I've put you in the Wedgwood bedchamber; Mrs. Holland will be happy to take you there."

At the mention of her name, a dour-faced housekeeper in mobcap and starched apron executed a stiff curtsy, then led Lady Fieldhurst up the curving staircase to the room that was to be hers for the next month.

As its name implied, the room was hung with the same blue shade as the china for which it was named, and trimmed out in woodwork painted a pristine white. It appeared neat and inviting even on a gray and rainy day; Lady Fieldhurst had no doubt that in sunshine it would be lovely. Her trunks had already been carried up, and an apple-cheeked maid bustled about the room hanging her gowns in the center of the clothes press and storing her undergarments in its drawers.

"I trust my lady will find everything to your liking," said the housekeeper. "If not, you have only to tell me, and I will be happy to rectify any omission."

The woman's accommodating words notwithstanding, Lady Fieldhurst had the distinct impression that any complaint about the room would not be happily received at all, but taken very much amiss.

"Thank you, Mrs. Holland," the viscountess replied, dismissing her with a nod. "This will do very well, I'm sure."

The housekeeper departed somewhat mollified, and as the maid completed her task, Lady Fieldhurst took stock of her surroundings. She noted with approval the Adam fireplace with its cheerful blaze, and the mahogany writing table adjacent to it. Glancing at the cheval mirror, however, she was considerably less pleased. The woman gazing back at her wore a stylish traveling costume of black kerseymere, but her skirts were creased from travel and spotted with raindrops, and her hem was two inches deep in mud.

She tugged at the black ribbons of her bonnet and tossed it onto the bed as she surveyed the damage to her coiffure. Her golden curls, though dry, were sadly flattened from her headgear, and would certainly have to be brushed out and pinned up again before dinner. She heaved a sigh at her own lack of foresight in neglecting to bring her lady's maid, but the girl was newly hired and Lady Fieldhurst was not yet entirely convinced as to her competence.

"Begging your pardon, your ladyship," said the maid, closing the doors of the clothes press, "but I've finished unpacking your trunks. Will there be anything else you'll be needing?"

"Only one thing," returned the viscountess, frowning at the damage to her crowning glory. "Is there a maid who could dress my hair before dinner?"

The maid's plump, plain face lit up. "Oh, I'd be pleased to do your ladyship's hair, right after I finish with Miss Hollingshead's."

"Excellent!" pronounced Lady Fieldhurst. "What time does the family dine?"

"Nine o'clock. We keep Town hours during the summer months," the maid added proudly.

"In that case, I must not keep you, for Miss Hollingshead will no doubt require your services very shortly. What is your name, pray?"

"Rose, my lady."

"Very well, Rose. That will be all."

"Yes, my lady." Rose bobbed a curtsy and exited the room.

Left to her own devices, Lady Fieldhurst divested herself of her damp pelisse and gown, then opened the double doors of the clothes press. Here was one small act of rebellion that her friend Lady Dunnington had heartily approved: after a scant two months of widowhood, she was going into half-mourning, exchanging her somber black crapes and bombazines for less funereal grays. She reached into the clothes press and withdrew a dinner gown of lustrous gray silk with a fine black stripe woven into the fabric, then laid it out almost lovingly on the bed. The garment might raise a few eyebrows despite its elegantly simple lines and modest *décolletage,* but the viscountess found the potential disapproval of her fellow guests less distasteful than the hypocrisy of mourning a philanderer whose violent death had almost sent her to the gallows. She was already the subject of gossip; she might as well give the tabbies something worth talking about. But even as she had made this momentous decision, she acknowledged her own cowardice in waiting to act upon it until she was well out of London.

Her thoughts were interrupted by a woman's voice coming from the next room and the sound of a door shutting a bit more forcefully than was strictly necessary.

"—Like a moonling, making sheep's eyes at Emma Hollingshead!"

"The lad is not yet two-and-twenty," a male voice responded more calmly. "Besides, Emma's a deuced pretty girl. I'd be more concerned if he *didn't* make sheep's eyes at her."

"Surely you have higher ambitions for your only son than to see him wed the daughter of a country squire!" objected the woman.

"And the granddaughter of a marquess on her mother's side," the man pointed out. "Added to the fact that their land borders ours, I can think of worse matches for the boy. But never you fear: Lady Anne has ambition enough to match your own. She'll give poor Robert his marching orders quickly enough." He chuckled at the prospect.

The woman, however, was not amused. "Just as she's given Mr. Meriwether his?" she retorted, her skepticism evident even through the dividing wall.

Lady Fieldhurst, cast in the rôle of unintentional eavesdropper, decided it was high time the people in the next room were made aware of her presence. She returned to the clothes press, opened the double doors, and shut them with sufficient force to make the heavy piece of furniture tremble. The couple next door immediately fell silent.

At half-past eight, having arrayed herself in the gray silk gown, Lady Fieldhurst left her room and made her way to the drawing room where, Rose had informed her, the family would gather before dinner. Rose's talents as a hairdresser had not disappointed: Julia's rejuvenated locks were swept high on her head, with little tendrils allowed to escape at the temples in order to soften a deceptively severe style. As she approached the drawing-room door, voices within the room alerted the viscountess to the fact that she was not the first arrival.

"You might have at least sent the carriage for him, Mama," complained a well-modulated contralto. "He can hardly be expected to walk all the way from the village in this weather."

"If he elects to remain at home rather than brave the elements, that is his decision," replied a cooler voice which Lady Fieldhurst recognized as that of her hostess. "If the weather proves too great a deterrent, then perhaps his affections are not so firmly engaged as you suppose. I need not remind you that he has made no attempt to speak to your father on the subject."

"No doubt he knows what sort of reception he might expect!"

It seemed to Lady Fieldhurst as if she were destined to be an eavesdropper will she or nill she. As she hovered in the hall wondering how best to make her presence known, Lady Anne Hollingshead addressed her daughter in conciliatory tones.

"Surely you cannot fault your father for that. With your birth and beauty, my dear, you might look a great deal higher. We only want you to look about before throwing yourself away on a penniless young man without birth or breeding—"

"Mama, how can you say such a thing? He is family!"

Lady Anne made a derisive sound which in a lesser personage would have been called a snort. "Wrong side of the blanket, or near enough as makes no odds."

Lady Fieldhurst decided it was high time to announce herself before she could make any more awkward discoveries about her fellow guests. She cleared her throat quite audibly, then sailed into the room. Two guilty countenances met her gaze for the briefest of moments before chagrin was masked by smiles.

"My dear Lady Fieldhurst, what a fetching frock," said Lady Anne. If the slightly raised eyebrow with which she regarded this creation was intended to shift Julia's attention to her own decision to cast off her blacks, it was singularly successful. However, her ladyship's voice held no note of censure as she urged her guest forward. "Do come and meet my elder daughter. Emma, my dear, make your curtsy to Lady Fieldhurst."

A dark-haired beauty of about twenty, Emma was less skilled than her mother in the social art of dissembling. Although she curtsied prettily enough, her heightened color and sparkling eyes betrayed her volatile emotional state.

"How do you do, Miss Hollingshead," responded Lady Fieldhurst, returning the younger woman's curtsy.

"I am sure Emma will have a great deal to ask you," continued Lady Anne, seemingly oblivious to her daughter's inner turmoil. "She is to be presented at court next spring and have her Season in London. I only hope she may enjoy a fraction of your own success. How well I remember your debut! You were quite the Toast of the Season, as I recall."

The viscountess, seeing Emma Hollingshead's face assume a mulish aspect, surmised that the approaching London Season was another bone of contention between mother and daughter. She could imagine few things more disagreeable than recounting her social successes—which had eventually culminated in a brilliant yet miserable marriage—to an obviously hostile audience. In fact, her debut had been a rather modest affair in Bath; it had been here that she had first been introduced to Frederick Bertram, Viscount Fieldhurst. The social triumph Lady Hollingshead recalled had taken place the following spring, after her whirlwind marriage. She remembered little of the court presentation itself, so fearful she had been of somehow disappointing the awe-inspiring gentleman who had swept her off her feet. It was perhaps inevitable that she had eventually done exactly that, and he had never let her forget it. She had no intention, however, of divulging these old hurts to women who were little more than strangers.

"It was all so long ago, I fear I can remember little beyond how absurd my high-waisted gown looked when worn over the hoops required at court," she told Miss Hollingshead apologetically.

"You are too modest by half," declared her hostess. "Surely you must remember more than that!"

"Now that I think of it, I recall how shockingly my head ached from the aigrette of ostrich plumes my abigail had fastened in my hair. I do believe the woman must have nailed the thing to my skull."

Although these less than glowing recollections found no favor with Lady Anne, they won a reluctant smile from her daughter, who was able to greet the next arrival with more composure. This proved to be a very young man dressed in the fashionable extravagance of the *Incroyable,* and Lady Fieldhurst wondered fleetingly if he might be the object of Miss Hollingshead's affections. A moment's reflection, however, was sufficient to remind her that one given to extremes of fashion would be unlikely to risk his finery by walking to dinner in a rainstorm; nor did the young man's raiment show any signs of his having done so. When a portly gentleman and a sharp-featured woman followed him into the room, the older man scolding the younger on the shirt points of his collar—the height of which made it impossible for him to turn his head—Julia realized that this was the quarreling couple in the bedchamber next to hers. The young dandy who was even now making a beeline for Emma Hollingshead could only be their son.

"Lady Fieldhurst, allow me to present Lord and Lady Kendall, and the Honourable Robert Kendall." Lady Anne performed the introductions with practiced grace. "The Kendalls are our nearest neighbors—except for the vicar, that is—and Lord Kendall is Justice of the Peace."

Lady Fieldhurst was surprised to discover that the Kendalls were in fact local, but before she had time to wonder at their occupation of one of the guest bedchambers, Lady Kendall supplied the explanation.

"I must thank you for allowing us the use of your guest chambers," she told her hostess. "I shudder to think what my gown would have looked like had I been obliged to pile in and out of a carriage in this rain. As for Robert," she added, scowling at her son, "I daresay he would never have consented to leave the house for fear of getting his coat wet."

Unfortunately, this rider was wasted. Young Mr. Kendall, listening with rapt attention to something Miss Hollingshead was saying, showed no sign of having heard his mother at all.

The drawing-room party was soon joined by others. Sir Gerald Hollingshead was the first of these, entering the room with the curious rigidity of the English country gentleman unwillingly stuffed into evening clothes. Next came the schoolroom set. Young Mr. Philip Hollingshead, on holiday from Eton, was almost as tall as a man, yet still possessed the smooth, rounded cheeks of childhood. His sister Susannah, the younger daughter of the household, was clad in demure white muslin with a pale blue sash, her unbound hair tied back with a matching blue ribbon. Lady Anne introduced her children with the air of one bestowing a rare treat, leading Lady Fieldhurst to surmise that they were not often granted the privilege of dining with their elders. Miss Susannah was accompanied by her governess, Miss Harriet Grantham, a once-handsome woman whose plum-colored satin gown had clearly seen better days. Hard on their heels came the butler to announce a pair of new arrivals.

"Mr. Cyril Danvers and Mr. Jasper Carrington," he intoned.

A short, rather frail man of sober attire and scholarly mien entered the room, accompanied by a raven-haired gentleman of indeterminate years whose swarthy complexion suggested a career spent in India or the West Indies. Any confusion Lady Fieldhurst might have felt as to which one was which was soon put to rest as Lady Anne greeted her guests.

"Mr. Danvers, how pleased I am that you could come," she said, offering her hand to the soberly dressed scholar. "I do hope you did not walk all the way from the vicarage. If the weather should bring on an attack of catarrh, I should never forgive myself."

"No, indeed, my lady! I should normally have spent such an inclement evening at home writing my sermon, but when Mr. Carrington offered me a place in his curricle, the prospect of good food and congenial company was too much to resist."

"In that case, Mr. Carrington, we stand in your debt," said Lady Anne, turning her attention to the dark gentleman.

"I assure you, my lady, the pleasure was all mine," he demurred.

Having exchanged pleasantries all around, the group indulged in idle chatter until the dinner gong sounded promptly at nine o'clock.

"Doubtless the weather proved too much for Mr. Meriwether," observed Sir Gerald, casting his elder daughter a glance that was not wholly without sympathy. "Shall we go?"

As Lady Fieldhurst was the highest ranking of the female guests, it was to her that he offered his arm. The others followed suit, pairing off according to rank, which left Miss Grantham to bring up the rear in solitary splendor. They had just reached the door when it burst open to admit a tall, bespectacled young man in outmoded evening wear which, besides being much worn at the knees and elbows, was decidedly damp. His windswept hair owed more to current weather conditions than to curling tongs, and his clocked stockings were liberally spattered with mud.

"Pray forgive my tardiness," he addressed the company in somewhat breathless accents. "The rain is letting up, but the road beyond the village is well nigh impassable in places, and the river is rising. I can only hope the bridge will not wash out."

"Indeed," said her hostess without enthusiasm, "Lady Fieldhurst, may I present Mr. Colin Meriwether, the curate and our distant cousin."

Color flooded Emma Hollingshead's glowing countenance, and she dropped Mr. Carrington's arm as if she would have flown to the curate's side. Good breeding restrained her from committing such a shocking *faux pas,* but her inclinations were clear enough, as evidenced by her mother's warning scowl as well as the glowering look bent upon the late arrival by the magnificent Mr. Kendall.

Lady Fieldhurst, although having sworn off men on her own account, had no objection to observing the romantic pursuits of others. Given a choice, she would put her money on Mr. Meriwether to carry the day; aside from Miss Hollingshead's obvious partiality, the young man's presence in the face of such discouragement suggested a strength of character sufficient to overcome any obstacles Lady Anne might place in his way.

In fact, decided the viscountess, her friend Lady Dunnington had been quite wrong in her assessment. The next four weeks should prove anything but dull.

Chapter 2

In Which a Dinner Party Draws to a Tragic Conclusion

The company now assembled, Mr. Meriwether offered the governess his arm with every indication of pleasure, and the entire party filed into the dining room. Lady Fieldhurst was seated at her host's right, as befitted her rank, and noted with some surprise that Mr. Meriwether occupied the corresponding position at the opposite end of the table; had the rules of precedence been strictly observed, Lord Kendall—not the curate—would have been given the place of honor at Lady Anne's right hand. The viscountess suspected that her hostess's reasoning had little to do with precedence, and everything to do with placing as much distance as possible between the ineligible young man and her eldest daughter. Indeed, so cleverly had she arranged the seating that the young lovers, seated on the same side of the table with both Mr. Robert Kendall and Miss Susannah Hollingshead between them, could not even make eye contact.

For her part, Lady Fieldhurst divided her attention between Sir Gerald on her left and Mr. Danvers on her right. As Sir Gerald had no liking for Town life and the vicar rarely visited London, the conversation was somewhat belabored. At length the viscountess abandoned all efforts at finding common ground for discussion and cast about in her mind for some acceptable excuse she might offer for seeking her bed. For the present, however, there was nothing for it but to encourage Sir Gerald to describe for her the glories of the Dales, and allow the vicar to express his regret that, due to the excessive rains of the past weeks, she was not seeing the Yorkshire countryside at its best.

Apparently Miss Susannah Hollingshead's thoughts were running along similar lines. "Will this rain never end?" she blurted out over the second course. "If the bridge washes out, everyone will have to stay the night—everyone but Mr. Danvers, anyway."

Miss Grantham, who clearly subscribed to the philosophy that children should not speak unless spoken to, shot her a warning frown. The vicar, however, answered her with paternal kindness. "Never fear, Miss Susannah. The river has not flooded in almost half a century."

"Tell me, Sir Gerald," said Lady Fieldhurst, in an effort to deflect the scold that clearly trembled on the governess's lips, "how is it that Hollingshead Place and the church are situated on one side of the river, while the village itself is positioned on the opposite bank?"

"You'd best ask Mr. Danvers about that," boomed her host genially, deferring to the vicar. "What he don't know about the district hasn't been thought of yet."

Mr. Danvers fairly beamed with pleasure. "You are too kind, Sir Gerald. But to answer your question, your ladyship, first of all, the river is not really a river at all, but merely a tributary that feeds into the River Nidd. As for the present location of the village, we have Sir Gerald's seventeenth-century ancestor, Sir Reginald Hollingshead, to thank for that. Sir Reginald was a sportsman—"

"Jolly good fellow, in fact," interpolated Sir Gerald.

"—And when he realized that the humblest villager had better access to trout fishing than he did, he moved the whole thing lock, stock and barrel, and extended his parkland to the water's edge. He was a superstitious man, however—I hesitate to call him a religious one—and he dared not tamper with the church for fear of divine retribution. It proved to be a wise decision on his part, for later in the century the river provided him with a natural defense against the Roundheads. Unlike so many parts of the country, neither the house nor the church was attacked, at least not with any degree of success."

"Sir Gerald was right," observed Lady Fieldhurst. "You seem to be exceptionally knowledgeable about the area."

"In truth, I fancy myself something of an historian," confessed the vicar, modesty obviously warring with pride. "I am in the process of writing a book about the history of the village and its church."

Across the table, Master Philip Hollingshead rolled his eyes toward the ceiling, and Lady Fieldhurst realized too late her error. The pained expressions on the faces around the table informed her that her fellow diners had already learned more than they wanted to know about the book from its proud author.

"I consider it my life's work," Mr. Danvers continued. "It has already grown to more than five hundred pages, and still it is not completely finished. It has been a fascinating exercise, studying the ancient church registries, reading about births, deaths, marriages—oh, I am reminded, Miss Grantham, I have something particular to ask you, if you would be so kind as to grant me an audience."

Color flooded the governess's cheeks, giving her something of the appearance of the young woman she had once been. "Why—why, certainly, Mr. Danvers. I should be honored."

Mr. Danvers turned back to Lady Fieldhurst. "I flatter myself that I am somehow bringing history to life—if I may borrow from the words of Ezekiel, I feel as if I am putting flesh back on the dry bones of those long dead."

"Yes, yes, but if we are to speak of flesh and bones," said Miss Grantham, addressing herself to the Justice of the Peace, "when do you intend to put a stop to all this cock-fighting,

Lord Kendall? It seems to me that such activities are a corrupting influence on young people."

"Balderdash!" protested Sir Gerald before the Justice of the Peace could answer. "Harmless bit of sport, if you ask me. I've been known to frequent the odd cock fight myself now and then, back in my salad days."

"I fear I must agree with Miss Grantham," concurred Mr. Danvers, momentarily distracted from the subject of his literary efforts. "I think I may understand their attraction, as the countryside offers few diversions for youthful high spirits. Unfortunately, aside from the cruelty of the sport itself, such gatherings invariably attract the basest sort of company and encourage all kinds of vice—gambling, drunkenness, and lewd behavior, to name only a few. I should not want to think of a son of mine participating in such goings-on."

This last was said with a pointed glance at Philip Hollingshead, who put up his chin and glared back at the vicar.

"He'd best get used to them, as most of 'em will be his tenants someday," said Sir Gerald.

"That may well be," acknowledged Lady Anne with a regal nod. "Still, you cannot wish your son and heir to develop a taste for low society."

"What, would you have the lad wrapped in cotton wool all his life?" continued Sir Gerald, his good humor unimpaired. "If we're to talk of low company, Kendall, what do you make of these gypsies camped hereabouts? Poaching in my Home Wood, stealing the vicar's chickens—"

"Indeed, yes," agreed Mr. Danvers, shaking his head. "I realize that we are called upon to aid the less fortunate, but while I would obey the biblical exhortation to give up my coat, and my cloak, too, I do draw the line at my best laying hen."

"Gypsies!" cried Miss Susannah, clapping her hands in glee.

"Oh, how romantic! How I should love to have my fortune told!"

"Susannah!" cried her mother, aghast. "What can Miss Grantham have been teaching you?"

Lord Kendall, Justice of the Peace, chuckled indulgently. "I'm afraid you would find very little romantic about them, Miss Susannah. They're a dirty, thieving lot, for the most part."

"Much as it grieves me to say such an uncharitable thing, I fear I must concur," said the vicar. "They have made such inroads into my poultry that only last week I was obliged to purchase a fowling piece and gunpowder."

"Surely you would not *shoot* them, Mr. Danvers?" protested Lady Kendall. "Better by far to let my husband deal with such matters."

"Shoot the gypsies?" echoed the vicar in some consternation. "No, no! I provided myself with a firearm merely for the purpose of frightening them off with a warning shot."

Lady Anne rose from her chair. "I think," she said with the faintest hint of disapproval in her voice, "that it is high time we ladies left you gentlemen alone with your port, where you may shoot all the gypsies you wish. Miss Grantham, I understand my daughter has been preparing a new piece upon the pianoforte. Is she ready to entertain us?"

"Indeed she is, my lady," said the governess hastily, painfully aware of having given offense by raising a sore subject at the dinner table. "Miss Susannah plays with great feeling, whatever she may lack in accuracy."

This assessment proved to be more than generous. Lady Fieldhurst, applauding politely after Miss Susannah's third piece, came to the conclusion that the girl either possessed a tin ear, or else her mind was still preoccupied with visions of gypsy fortune-tellers. Nevertheless, the viscountess seated herself beside the governess on the sofa and complimented her on her charge's enthusiastic (she could find no more complimentary term without resorting to outright falsehood) performance.

All in all, it was a relief when the gentlemen joined the ladies in the drawing room and the concert drew to a close. Nor, it seemed, was she the only one who found it so: Emma Hollingshead observed Colin Meriwether's entrance with a smile of eager anticipation. The curate lost no time in claiming the chair beside hers, thus beating out a sullen Mr. Kendall for the honor. Likewise Mr. Danvers sought out Miss Grantham, who blushed like a schoolgirl at the vicar's approach. Lady Fieldhurst, seeing that her presence was no longer required or even wanted, murmured a vague excuse and started to rise.

"No, no, my lady, you need not get up," protested Mr. Danvers. "I only wanted to beg a favor of Miss Grantham."

"Yes?" asked the governess breathlessly. "What is it?"

"Would you do me the honor—" He reached into his coat and drew out a thick parcel wrapped in brown paper and tied with string. "—Of checking my manuscript for errors? I should very much value your opinion."

"Your—your manuscript?" Miss Grantham made no move to accept the package he offered, but stared blindly at it through pale eyes struggling to blink back tears. Lady Fieldhurst, seeing that quite a different sort of question had been expected, plunged hastily into the breach.

"Why, Miss Grantham, you must be a highly skilled grammarian! After hearing Mr. Danvers discuss his book at dinner, I suspect he would not entrust his life's work to just anyone."

"No, indeed," agreed Mr. Danvers, blissfully unaware of having dashed a lady's last hope of matrimony. "In fact, I was reluctant to request such a favor, knowing that your young charge can be quite a handful—though I am certain Miss Susannah is a good girl, merely high-spirited as young people so often are. Still, since you are the most qualified of all my acquaintance for such a task, I fear my own selfishness won out over any fear of adding to your responsibilities."

Miss Grantham, twisting her handkerchief in trembling hands, appeared somewhat mollified. "Well, if I do say so myself, my own dear governess used to say that I had an exceptional grasp of the intricacies of language."

By the time she bade Miss Susannah and Master Philip say their goodbyes and led them back to the schoolroom, she had consented to read the vicar's manuscript and had borne it away with the air of one presented with a precious gift.

With the departure of the children Sir Gerald summoned a footman to set up card tables, and Lady Fieldhurst was solicited to help make up a set for whist.

"I fear I am not much of a card player," she cautioned Mr. Meriwether, her partner, as she seated herself opposite him at one of the tables. "My late husband always said I hadn't the head for games of skill."

"Nor have I, my lady, so I daresay we shall deal extremely together," he said with a smile.

Their opponents were Mr. Carrington and Lady Anne, and once again the viscountess noted that lady's skill in pairing her daughter with Lord Kendall at the next table. She wondered fleetingly which her hostess found the most objectionable—the young man's dubious birth, or his lack of fortune. For her part, Lady Fieldhurst might have found much to be said in favor of the curate's suit, had not her own marriage permanently soured her on that institution. Modesty, certainly, must be attributed to him, for in spite of his disavowals, he played his cards with quiet intelligence. Likewise courtesy, for nothing in his bearing toward the other players gave the least indication that he would much prefer playing at the other table. As for his manner toward Miss Hollingshead, so restrained was he that Lady Fieldhurst might have supposed that young lady's feelings to be unrequited, had she not witnessed for the briefest moment the expression of wordless longing in his eyes when they rested upon her.

They had played two rubbers for penny points when Mr. Danvers, partnering Lady Kendall at the next table, glanced at the clock over the mantel.

"Dear me, half past eleven already!" he exclaimed. "How quickly time passes when one spends it so pleasantly among friends."

Mr. Carrington, taking his cue, laid his cards faceup on the table and made as if to rise. "I shall have the carriage brought round at once."

"No, no, you need not trouble yourself," protested the vicar. "Since Mr. Meriwether assures us that the rain has let up, there is no reason why I should not walk."

"None at all, save for a muddy road and a lack of pattens," put in Sir Gerald. "But there's no need for Mr. Carrington to leave us just yet. I can send you home in my own carriage."

"Or you can ride with us," added Lord Kendall, hoisting himself to his feet. "It may be a bit crowded, given the number of trunks Robert judges necessary to transport his toilette, but I daresay we can shove up enough to make room for one more. Or we can leave some of his bits and pieces here for the night, and he may fetch them in the morning."

Robert Kendall's mouth worked in protest over this cavalier dismissal of his wardrobe, but words failed him.

Mr. Danvers, however, would not be dissuaded. "I should not wish to put any one of my flock to any inconvenience, lest you take a chill and miss Sunday services. I wonder, though, if you will bear me company as far as the door, Sir Gerald? An issue of some importance has arisen which I need to discuss with you."

"Certainly, certainly!" boomed the baronet, pushing back his chair and heaving himself to his feet. "Repairs to the church roof again, I daresay. Well, the whole thing may jolly well need replacing after this monsoon—probably leaking like a sieve."

Sir Gerald returned a few minutes later, *sans* the vicar. Lady Anne, studying the cards in her hand, looked up as he entered the room. "You look worried. Are you quite certain it was wise to let him go alone?"

The baronet shook his grizzled head. "No stopping the fellow, my dear. I tried to get him to wait while I had the carriage brought 'round, but there's no persuading these scholarly types—once they take an idea into their heads, you can't beat it out with a stick."

The card game ran its course in silence. The party broke up soon afterwards, any pleasure in the evening diminished, perhaps, by the thought of the vicar slogging home through the mud. One by one, the guests said their goodbyes and departed, until at last only Lady Fieldhurst and the Hollingsheads remained. Her long day of travel had by this time caught up with her, and she wondered how long it might be until she could politely take leave of her host and hostess and seek her bed.

"I vow, I am worn to the bone," declared Emma Hollingshead, yawning behind her gloved hand. "I hope you will not think me rude, Lady Fieldhurst, if I say goodnight."

The viscountess was quick to seize her opportunity. "On the contrary, I find it an excellent notion."

She accompanied the younger woman up the stairs, but they had scarcely reached the landing when the jingle of harness and the crunch of carriage wheels on gravel announced a late arrival.

"Good heavens," muttered Lady Anne. "Who can that be at such an hour?"

The footman, who had been engaged in clearing away the playing cards and putting away the tables, abandoned this task long enough to open the front door. Lord Kendall burst into the room, considerably the worse for the mud splattering his stockings. "I fear it is just as Mr. Meriwether predicted," he said without preamble. "The bridge is out."

The next half hour flew by in a flurry of activity. Lady Anne, prophesying that all the guests save the vicar would return soon enough, summoned the housekeeper and ordered five additional bedchambers prepared. The Kendall family's return was followed within minutes by that of Mr. Carrington. Since Mr. Danvers did not have to cross the bridge, he was not looked for, it being assumed by all that he should have reached his vicarage safely enough by now. There remained only the curate unaccounted for.

"What can be keeping Mr. Meriwether?" Lady Anne wondered aloud. "You don't suppose he could have fallen into the river?"

Lady Fieldhurst suspected her hostess would not be devastated should that prove to be the case.

"Now that you mention it," said Lord Kendall, "I don't recall passing him on the road. I trust no harm has come to the lad."

"I think it far more likely that he stopped by the vicarage," put in Lady Fieldhurst. In fact, she was not well enough acquainted with the curate to venture an informed opinion of what sort of action he might take, but she felt that Miss Hollingshead might be in need of reassurance. Glancing around the room, however, she realized that her efforts in that direction were wasted; Emma Hollingshead was nowhere to be seen.

"I'm going to take a lantern and have a look at that bridge," announced Sir Gerald. "I'll keep an eye out for him."

After rooms had been prepared and assigned, there seemed to be little left to do. One by one, the guests drifted upstairs to their allotted chambers, Lord Kendall requesting to be awakened regardless of the hour, should it prove that some misfortune had indeed befallen the curate. Lady Fieldhurst followed their example, only too grateful to reach the privacy of her bedchamber. She could not deny some concern for Mr. Meriwether's safety, however, and so after unpinning her hair and exchanging her gray silk gown for a white muslin nightrail and a wrapper of pink satin, she walked over to the window, drew back the curtain and pushed open the casement.

The rain had indeed stopped, but the night air was heavy and damp with the promise of more to come. Lightning occasionally lit up the sky to the east, and muted thunder rumbled in the distance. There was no sign of the curate, nor indeed of any other living creature. She turned away, but even as she reached for the casement, a movement of shadow caught her eye, followed by a glimpse of red in the garden below. Her hand stayed; she watched as a dark shape detached itself from the shrubbery.

A moment later, Emma Hollingshead was safely in the arms of her lover.

Julia knew she should draw back; she was, after all, intruding on a private moment. Still, it was rather like watching a play. Young lovers, no matter how sincere their devotion, were really quite painfully alike. In a way, it might be better if they were never allowed to marry, for then their romantic illusions need never be shattered by harsh reality. This thought led, not unnaturally, to unpleasant memories of her own marriage.

And then, abruptly, she was recalled to the present by the sound of her own name.

"—Lady Fieldhurst to dazzle me with tales of her own brilliant Season." The bitterness in Emma Hollingshead's voice was audible as it drifted up from the garden below. "Can you imagine? A woman who killed her own husband—"

"Hush, my love, and listen to yourself," Mr. Meriwether chided her gently. "Lady Fieldhurst did *not* kill her husband, as you well know."

"You are right, of course," conceded Miss Hollingshead, deflated. "But you cannot know what it is like to live in this house, feeling as if the whole world is conspiring to tear us apart. You can have no idea!"

He chuckled. "I do, actually. But I feel you must acquit Lady Fieldhurst as a co-conspirator. I think it very likely that her ladyship had no idea for what purpose she was invited."

"Perhaps," Miss Hollingshead admitted, albeit somewhat grudgingly. "But it really doesn't matter, for I shall never give you up, no matter what anyone may say!"

"Hold fast to that thought, my love, and be patient. I have a plan which I hope will allow us to be together very soon as man and wife forever."

"Oh, what is it?"

He hesitated. "I dare not say more, for fear of raising hopes that may yet be dashed. Only trust me, and try to be strong."

"I will, for your sake," she vowed with feeling. "And when Mama and Lady Fieldhurst describe the delights of a London Season, I shall pretend to be persuaded."

"Good girl! Although, since her ladyship's marriage turned out so very badly, she might prove to be a valuable ally."

"If only I can be allied to you, my darling, I shall need no other."

His reply was muffled as the two shadows merged into one.

At the end of a protracted farewell, the lovers went their separate ways. Emma re-entered the house through a side door, spilling out a shaft of yellow light which illuminated the curate's profile ever so briefly before he vanished into the shadows beyond.

Staring down into the empty garden, Julia resolved to make her excuses and escape from this ill-assorted gathering as soon as the bridge was repaired. Whatever her sympathy for the star-crossed lovers—and she was surprised to discover she *was* sympathetic to their plight in spite of the less than happy ending of her own whirlwind romance—she had no intention of becoming embroiled in a quarrel that was none of her concern.

But even were she to leave, where would she go? *Not* to the dower house and her mother-in-law, that much was certain. Nor did she have any desire to visit Fieldhurst House, where she would be obliged to watch her late husband's cousin play at being a viscount. London was unbearable in summer, while Brighton—as she had pointed out to her friend Emily, Lady Dunnington—was far too festive for a lady supposedly in mourning. She thought of Emily, enjoying the frivolities of Brighton with her latest paramour, and of Lord Rupert Latham, who but for the murder of Lord Fieldhurst would now be her own lover. In truth, she did not regret his loss any more than she did that of her husband. She sighed, wondering if perhaps there was something wrong with her as a woman. In the weeks since she had been cleared of suspicion in her husband's murder, she had been aware of a certain restlessness, a lack of purpose which she could neither understand nor overcome. It was this, more than anything else that had driven her northward to Yorkshire, but even this had been in vain: it seemed there was no relief to be found here, either.

A sharp crack, unheralded by the flash of light which usually precedes such outbursts, startled her from her reverie. She ducked back into her room and shut the window, then tossed her wrapper over the back of a chair and extinguished the single candle beside her bed. She settled herself comfortably beneath the covers and was just surrendering to Morpheus's embrace when a sudden commotion outside dragged her ruthlessly back to consciousness.

"Sir Gerald! Your ladyship!" shouted a voice below, while someone pounded on the front door as if attempting to break it down. "Open the door! The vicarage is burning!"

All thoughts of sleep flown, Lady Fieldhurst leaped from her bed, raced to the window, and looked out. On the horizon, thick smoke billowed over the treetops, eerily lit with an orange glow. By the time she had thrown on the nearest gown to hand, hastily scraped back her hair, and hurried downstairs, every able-bodied man on the estate had been recruited to help battle the blaze. Such artificial distinctions as rank were set aside as Sir Gerald and Lord Kendall worked side by side with the lowliest stable hands and pot boys to extinguish the flames. Even Mr. Kendall made no mention of the potential damage to his coat, but donned borrowed oilskins and hurried after the others.

Inside, the ladies of the house descended upon the kitchens to assist the staff in brewing the tea and coffee that would be needed to fortify the fire fighters upon their return. The kitchen was warm and dry, save for a damp cloak of scarlet worsted which hung from a hook beside the door. Julia recognized it as the one Emma Hollingshead had worn for her assignation and hoped Lady Anne would be too distracted to notice it.

"Strange to think of anything burning on such a night as this, wet as it is," Lady Kendall said, tying a coarse cotton apron over the elegant indigo crape she had worn to dinner.

The cook looked up from slicing a loaf of day-old bread for sandwiches. "I'll wager 'twas the lightning what did it. 'Tis a beastly night, and no mistake."

"I hope poor Mr. Danvers had time to escape the house before the flames spread," said Lady Anne, in between giving orders to her staff. "I confess, I am concerned. I should have thought he would have come to us straightaway."

As if on cue, the heavy tread of a boot sounded just outside the kitchen door. It opened a moment later to admit, not the vicar, but a damp and windblown Mr. Meriwether, who blinked at the sight of the entire female population of Hollingshead Place bustling about the kitchen.

"Colin!" cried Miss Hollingshead, bursting into overwrought tears. "Where have you been? I've been imagining the most dreadful things!"

He blinked in bewilderment. "Imagining—but why should you? What on earth has happened here?"

"The vicarage is on fire," explained Lady Anne, regarding him with narrowed eyes. "Surely you must have seen the smoke?"

Mr. Meriwether, who had stripped off his greatcoat and hung it on a hook next to the scarlet cloak, froze with one hand still grasping its worn collar. "And Mr. Danvers—?"

"We don't know," continued his kinswoman. "He may well be helping the other men to put out the flames. We cannot know for certain until they return. When I heard you outside, I thought perhaps it was they."

"No, but of course I must do anything in my power to help." He shrugged back into the cloak he had just removed. "If there is any sign of him, I shall send word."

The ladies agreed readily to this plan (save for Miss Hollingshead, who was loath to let him go) but no word came. In fact, there was no sign of Mr. Danvers at all until well after dawn, when Lord Kendall had sufficient light to locate the vicar's charred body among the smoldering remains of what had once been his study.

It was a somber company that gathered in the breakfast room several hours later. Miss Grantham snuffled incessantly into her handkerchief, and even the irrepressible Miss Susannah Hollingshead was strangely subdued. Master Philip Hollingshead pouted over his parents' failure to awaken him so that he might assist in the rescue efforts ("the most excitement we've had around here in years!"), and Mr. Kendall, now that the crisis had passed, was inclined to complain about the smell of smoke clinging to his coat.

"I daresay my valet will never get it out," he grumbled.

"In case you have forgotten, Robert, a man is dead," Lord Kendall censured his son and heir. "Surely the condition of your coat is irrelevant, under the circumstances."

"Pray do not be too hard on him, my lord," protested Mr. Meriwether, coming to the younger man's defense. "I believe it is not unusual for the mind, when confronted with tragedy, to focus instead on the trivial."

The Honourable Robert, however, found his rival's show of support even more objectionable than his father's scold. "Trivial?" he echoed, sneering at the curate's threadbare garments. "I am pleased to know you find my clothing of so little importance. I daresay if I dressed as you do, I should feel likewise. But I think we know what occupies your mind in this time of crisis."

"Robert—" growled his father.

Mr. Meriwether frowned. "I think it is perhaps best that I fail to take your meaning," he said, then turned back to the older man. "Lord Kendall, how extensive is the damage to the vicarage? Can anything be salvaged, do you suppose?"

"Yes, you'll want to move in as soon as possible, I don't doubt," sneered Mr. Kendall. "But how fortuitous that you should succeed to the living just before Miss Hollingshead goes to London for her Season. One might almost call Mr. Danvers's death providential."

"Robert!" barked his father.

"You will kindly leave Miss Hollingshead's name out of this discussion," the usually gentle Mr. Meriwether ground out through clenched teeth.

Miss Hollingshead, pushing a forkful of buttered eggs about

on her plate, acknowledged neither of her suitors, but focused her attention instead on the Justice of the Peace. "What is to be done now, Lord Kendall?"

"With the body, you mean?" His lordship gave his son one last glowering look before fixing gentler eyes on Miss Hollingshead. "Nothing at all, at least for the nonce. The coroner must be notified, of course, but with the bridge out, there's no way to send word to him, and no way for him to reach us even if we could—not that we don't already know how Danvers died, God rest his soul."

"Waste of time, then," declared Sir Gerald. "He'll need to be put underground long before the bridge will be repaired."

Lord Kendall shook his head. "He can't be buried before the coroner's seen him—can't be buried now in any case, not after all this rain. The churchyard's on low ground—too saturated by half."

"What of the funeral, then?" asked Lady Anne, frowning, no doubt, at Mr. Danvers's thoughtlessness in dying at such an inopportune time.

"It'll have to be postponed until things dry out a bit. In the meantime, Sir Gerald, if some of your men can construct a coffin, I suggest we let the poor old fellow rest in the church."

"The vestry," put in Mr. Meriwether. "It will be cooler there."

Mr. Kendall muttered something under his breath, the only intelligible words of which were "taking charge already."

Lady Fieldhurst's shocked gaze traveled from the sullen dandy to the curate, whose tightened jaw betrayed his awareness of the insult even though he forbore to make any more direct acknowledgement.

It was not until late the following day, after a temporary bridge had been erected over the swollen stream, that the party finally took its leave of Sir Gerald and Lady Anne. Lady Fieldhurst, having by this time lost all inclination for socializing, sought refuge in her bedchamber, where she pondered the events of the last forty-eight hours. She was not quite certain why she should be so overset by the death of a comparative stranger, but she suspected it was as much the air of suspicion and accusation that hung over the house's inhabitants as the tragedy itself. Without a doubt, Robert Kendall's sly insinuations had worked their mischief: Lady Anne's demeanor toward the curate was even chillier than before, and when Mr. Meriwether bade his sweetheart goodbye, so distant was Miss Hollingshead's demeanor that they might have been no more than chance-met strangers. Lord Kendall regarded first his son and then Mr. Meriwether with measuring, speculative looks, while even Miss Susannah eyed her elders with wide, haunted eyes. Did the denizens of Hollingshead Place set so much store by the jealous pique of a rejected suitor that they would suspect foul play in what was surely no more than a tragic accident? And yet she could not quite forget the romantic scene enacted in the garden below her window, and the curate's ambiguous assurances. *I have a plan which I hope will allow us to be together very soon . . . I dare not say more . . .* She wished there were someone to whom she might voice her concerns, but she was not sufficiently well acquainted with her hostess to broach so delicate a subject.

Certainly she was no stranger to untimely death; it had been only two months since her husband's murder had plunged her and her nearest (if not dearest) kin into a similar web of doubt and suspicion. Yet there had been one person upon whom she had come to depend more and more throughout those dark days. It was perhaps inevitable, then, that her thoughts should now turn to a lanky young man with a slightly crooked nose and curling brown hair tied back in an unfashionable queue. Obeying a sudden impulse, she drew a sheet of writing paper and a quill pen from the mahogany writing table and wrote a short message. She reread it, frowning, then added a rather lengthy postscript, folded the letter, and sealed it with a wafer. She dipped her quill once more into the inkwell, and directed the missive to the attention of Mr. John Pickett, Bow Street Public Office, Number 4 Bow Street, London.

Chapter 3

In Which John Pickett Assumes an Incognito

John Pickett, at four-and-twenty the youngest Runner on the Bow Street force, stared at the letter in his increasingly shaky hands and read it through four times before fully comprehending its meaning. He had not seen Lady Fieldhurst in two long months, although not a day had gone by when he had not thought of her. He had even called on her in Berkeley Square just the week before, on the pretext of returning a handkerchief that belonged to her. He had paced the perimeter of the square three times before summoning the courage to knock on the door. When the butler had informed him that she was no longer in Town, and offered to see the handkerchief returned to its rightful owner, so bitter had been his disappointment that he meekly surrendered his prize without argument, giving up in the process his only excuse for seeing her again.

And now, miraculously, she had sent for him. It remained only for him to persuade Mr. Colquhoun, the magistrate, to allow him to travel to Yorkshire to investigate a death that might have been no more than a tragic accident. And then there was the matter of her ladyship's postscript:

As I am the houseguest of Sir Gerald and Lady Anne Hollingshead, the presence of a Bow Street Runner in the vicinity at my request would render my position extremely awkward. Would it be possible for you to investigate in some unofficial capacity, without revealing your profession? I realize this is ask-

ing a great deal of you, and confess I have no idea how such a thing might be accomplished except to say that I have every confidence in your intelligence and resourcefulness, having been the beneficiary of both.

For such a commendation, he would have assured her ladyship of his ability to fly to the moon, if she so desired.

Great tact would be needed, however, in gaining Mr. Colquhoun's permission. The magistrate was well aware that his most junior Runner's interest in the viscountess went beyond the purely professional, and he was not shy about letting his disapproval be known. Pickett waited until the magistrate had heard his last case for the day, then approached the bench with a careful air of nonchalance. "Mr. Colquhoun?"

"Yes, Pickett?" the magistrate asked, without looking up from the papers he was studying. "What is it?"

Pickett took a deep breath and plunged into speech. "When I was first promoted from the foot patrol, you told me that, as a Bow Street Runner, I might have the opportunity to supplement my wages by accepting private commissions."

"Yes, what of it?"

"I—As it happens, sir, such an occasion has arisen. I received a letter from Yorkshire in today's post."

Mr. Colquhoun removed his spectacles and regarded Pickett from beneath bushy white brows. Pickett's words, chosen with such care, were innocent enough, but the gleam in his brown eyes and the faint flush on his cheeks betrayed him. "Indeed?" queried the magistrate. "May I see the letter?"

"No—no need to trouble yourself, sir," stammered Pickett, stuffing the letter into the inside pocket of his brown serge coat. "It concerns a fire near the village of Kendall—"

Mr. Colquhoun leaned forward across the bench and held out his hand. "The letter, if you please."

Pickett, seeing resistance was futile, surrendered her ladyship's missive, and fidgeted silently while the magistrate examined its contents.

"Lady Fieldhurst," he said, when he had reached the end. "Tell me, Pickett, would this be the same Lady Fieldhurst whose husband was murdered a couple of months ago?"

"In-indeed, it would," Pickett confessed, then belatedly added, "sir."

Mr. Colquhoun's eyebrows drew together across the bridge of his nose in a formidable frown. "I am extremely reluctant to encourage you in this obsession."

Pickett bristled at the word. "One can admire a lady without being obsessed!"

"I beg your pardon. Doubtless you have taken to strolling about Berkeley Square for the sake of your health."

Pickett went crimson with mortification. "You had me followed!"

"You overestimate your own importance, sirrah! In fact, I was invited to dinner at the home of Sir Bartholomew Digby. As luck would have it, he lives in Berkeley Square, almost directly opposite the Fieldhurst town house. I saw you."

"It was a one-time occurrence," confessed Pickett, deflated. "On the night of his lordship's murder, I inadvertently put the lady's handkerchief into my coat pocket while examining the body. I went to Berkeley Square that evening with the intention of returning it to her."

"Very gallant of you, I'm sure. I trust her ladyship was suitably grateful?"

"I wouldn't know, sir. I was obliged to leave it with her butler. Her ladyship had gone to Yorkshire." Seeing that the magistrate was not convinced, Pickett returned to the more pressing matter at hand. "Whatever my feelings for the lady, and however much you may disapprove of them, you cannot deny that she deserves no less from Bow Street than any other British citizen might expect."

"No, you have me there," acknowledged the magistrate. "Lady Fieldhurst has requested a Runner, and so a Runner she shall have. I'll send Foote in your stead."

"You can't do that!"

As soon as the words were out, Pickett realized he had overstepped the mark rather badly. Mr. Colquhoun's bushy white brows arched toward his hairline.

"I was not aware that I took my orders from you, Mr. Pickett."

"No, sir. I beg your pardon. But—"

"Well?" prompted the magistrate, when Pickett hesitated. "But what?"

"She sent for *me*."

"Selected specially, no doubt, from her ladyship's vast acquaintance of Bow Street Runners," said Mr. Colquhoun, his voice heavy with irony.

"She—" He stood a little taller, struggling to suppress the singularly foolish smile that threatened to break free at the memory of her ladyship's words. "She has 'every confidence in my intelligence and resourcefulness,' sir."

"Hmmm, yes, she did empty the butter boat over your head, didn't she?" grunted the magistrate, scowling down at the letter in his hands. "And how, pray, do you expect to conduct an investigation without letting anyone know what you are about?"

"I've been thinking about that, and I have an idea."

"Somehow I rather suspected you would," Mr. Colquhoun observed dryly. "No, Pickett, if you take this sort of fulsome praise at face value, I am all the more justified in dampening your pretensions. I would do no less for one of my own sons, should he form an unsuitable attachment."

"I am flattered by your concern, sir, but I have no need of it.

I am four-and-twenty, and have been on my own for these past ten years."

"Believe me, John, I am well aware of that."

The magistrate's voice held a hint of bitterness, and Pickett found himself in the unaccustomed position of wishing to reassure his mentor. "I don't blame you for what you did, sir. A less merciful judge might have sentenced him to the gallows."

"Yes, yes, all this is neither here nor there," Mr. Colquhoun growled, impatient to abandon a subject which had become uncomfortably personal. "Go about your business, boy, and send Foote to me."

"Yes, sir."

Pickett made no further protest, but the light in his eyes was extinguished, and his disappointment was etched in every line of his drooping shoulders and bowed head. Mr. Colquhoun's gaze followed him as he crossed the room to the opposite corner, where a Runner a dozen years his senior sat puffing on a pipe and conversing with a red-waistcoated member of the foot patrol. As the junior Runner approached his more senior fellow, however, Mr. Colquhoun's eyes grew glazed. The tall young man vanished, and in his place stood the gawky, skinny youth whose father would soon be transported to Botany Bay.

"Oh, all right," barked the magistrate, as if the words had been torn from his unwilling throat. "If the only alternative is to see you moping about like a sick calf, then I'd best send you packing, and good riddance!"

Pickett froze in mid-step, his eyes widening as comprehension dawned. "You mean it, sir?"

"I do—God help me."

Pickett returned to the bench with a much sprightlier step and, seizing the magistrate's hand, began to pump it vigorously. "Thank you, sir! Thank you! You won't regret it, I promise!" he added before hurrying away to prepare for his journey.

"Now, *that* I beg leave to doubt," muttered Mr. Colquhoun, and turned back to his papers.

In spite of his impatience to depart for Yorkshire, Pickett did not head straight for his lodgings in Drury Lane, but instead set out on foot for Berkeley Square. In contrast to his last visit to that exclusive Mayfair locale, he did not on this occasion pace the square in nervous anticipation. Indeed, he did not approach the front door at all, but descended the curving stairs to the service entrance below street level. He knocked on the door, and a moment later it was opened by a rosy-cheeked chambermaid in a starched apron and mobcap.

"Lord, it's Mr. Pickett, from Bow Street!" she exclaimed, batting her eyes at the unexpected caller. "What might you be wanting, sir?"

"I should like to have a word with the footman Thomas, if you please."

The maid looked less than delighted with this information but bade Pickett step inside while she fetched Thomas.

"Why, Mr. Pickett, fancy seeing you again," said the footman, joining him a short time later. "What brings you here?"

Pickett took a deep breath. "I should like to ask you a small favor, Thomas. I want you to teach me how to be a footman."

An hour later, he set out for his hired lodgings in Drury Lane with Thomas's instructions ringing in his ears and Thomas's second-best livery wrapped neatly in brown paper. Before he reached his destination, however, he was accosted by a pert female in a garish purple bonnet and a faded bodice cut far too low over her plump bosom.

"Heigh-ho, John Pickett, have you grown too high-and-mighty to speak to an old friend?" Her brown eyes fastened with childlike avarice onto the brown paper package under his arm. "What's that?"

"A suit of livery." He fought to suppress a mischievous grin. "I'm going into domestic service, Lucy."

"Never say you're leaving Bow Street!"

Conflicting emotions chased one another across Lucy's expressive countenance as she weighed the ramifications of this statement. One of the many prostitutes who walked the streets surrounding Covent Garden, Lucy had considered Pickett her exclusive property ever since he had first arrested her for the lucrative practice of picking her client's pocket while he slept. Pickett's persistent refusal to consummate the relationship (for a fee, of course) was a constant source of frustration to her.

"No, I'm not leaving Bow Street." He took her arm as they crossed St. Martin's Lane, but released it as soon as they reached the pavement on the other side; it would not do to give her any encouragement. "At least not permanently. I'll be working incognito for a time."

Lucy pouted a little at the loss of his escort. "Well, I don't doubt you'll look fine as fivepence, all dressed up and with your hair powdered white—or will you wear a periwig?"

"I'll powder it," said Pickett, whose devotion to Lady Fieldhurst stopped short of shaving off his shoulder-length brown locks. He frowned, remembered Thomas's convoluted instructions. "I only hope I can manage it."

"I'll help you," offered Lucy, slipping her hand through the curve of his arm. "I'll come over before dawn, and do your hair and cook your breakfast, too. Lud, it'll be just like I was your left-hand wife!"

Pickett stepped backwards so quickly he almost lost his balance and tumbled into the street. "I won't be there, Lucy. I'm going to Yorkshire. Her ladyship has sent for me."

Lucy's eyes narrowed in sudden suspicion. "What ladyship?"

"Lady Fieldhurst."

"O-ho! So it's Lady Fieldhurst again, is it?" Lucy's words were mocking, but her expression was petulant. "Does she want you for her fancy-man?"

"Good God, no!" Pickett flushed scarlet. "Her ladyship has no interest in me at all beyond the professional."

Lucy arched a knowing eyebrow. "More's the pity, hmm? I know exactly how you feel. Only *some* men don't even have a professional interest in me, if you know what I mean. How long will you be gone?"

"I don't know. Until I can solve her ladyship's problem, or until Mr. Colquhoun recalls me to Bow Street, I suppose." Seeing she was still inclined to sulk, he added more gently, "I can't pass up an opportunity like this."

"No, you was wanting an excuse to see her ladyship again, wasn't you?"

Pickett winced at her too-keen perception. "It's more than that. I have a chance to earn money beyond my usual wages."

"Why should I care?" Lucy muttered with a disdainful sniff. "It's not like I'll ever see a farthing of it."

Pickett sighed. He was genuinely fond of Lucy and did not want to hurt her, but neither did he want to impregnate her or contract the pox from her. Still, it was not Lucy's fault that he had set his sights on a woman so far above him that the lady would no doubt laugh at the idea of any relationship between them—in the unlikely event that any such idea should occur to her at all.

"Look, Lucy, when I get back, I'll take you to the theater. We'll sit right up front, where the others in the pit won't block your view."

"Really?" exclaimed Lucy, all smiles once more. "You promise?"

"I promise."

"You'll hurry back?"

"I'll do my best," Pickett assured her, knowing it was a lie even as he spoke the words. The longer this case took, the happier he would be, so long as Lady Fieldhurst was there. Prompted by the combined forces of pity, affection, and a guilty conscience, he bent and gave Lucy a quick peck on the cheek. "In the meantime, try not to get yourself tossed into Bridewell while I'm gone."

He arrived at the village of Kendall via stagecoach some four days later. He collected his belongings from the boot and, discovering an obliging farmer headed in the same direction, begged a ride on this worthy's cart as far as the bridge. Upon being deposited at this destination, Pickett gave the farmer sixpence for his pains, then hoisted the valise onto his shoulder and trudged up the muddy track toward Hollingshead Place. He had not gone far before he came upon the stone church and, beyond it, the blackened remains of the vicarage. He paused. He would want a closer look, but it would not do to arrive at Hollingshead Place smelling of smoke. No, his investigation would have to wait. First, he must get himself safely installed in the servants' quarters. To that end, he cast one last look at the ruined vicarage, then set off toward the big house, where he soon presented himself at the service entrance.

It was opened to him by a buxom lass wearing the mobcap and apron of the kitchen maid. She looked him up and down appreciatively for a long moment, taking in every detail from the unfashionably shallow crown of his hat to his scuffed and muddied boots. Having completed this inspection, she inquired in unrefined accents, "What can I do for you, ducks?"

"How do you do? I'm John Pickett, footman to Lady Fieldhurst—"

"Footman, eh?" She leaned against the doorjamb, crossing her arms beneath her ample bosom. "Aye, I trow you'd know just how to serve a lady."

Pickett colored, but plunged gamely on. "I've just arrived from London. If you could inform her ladyship—"

"Molly!" interrupted a sharp female voice.

The kitchen maid gave a guilty start and turned to face the speaker, all traces of coquetry vanished. "Beggin' your pardon, Mrs. Holland, I meant no harm—"

"I know exactly what you meant, my girl, and it'll get you in trouble one of these days, mark my words."

With this warning—or was it a threat?—the speaker moved into Pickett's range of vision. Had the maid's deferential manner not identified Mrs. Holland as the housekeeper, the older woman's attire must surely have done so, although this specimen of the breed appeared to have little in common with the plump, motherly woman who performed the same office for Lady Fieldhurst. This formidable female's starched black bombazine was scarcely more severe than the expression with which she regarded him, as if she suspected him of coming northward for the sole purpose of seducing the serving girls under her charge.

"And you are?"

"John Pickett, of—" He hauled himself up short just before saying *of Bow Street*. "Of London, ma'am. Footman to Lady Fieldhurst. Her ladyship sent for me."

Her coldly appraising gaze gave him to understand that he had been weighed in the balances and found wanting. "If Lady Fieldhurst is displeased with the service she has received from Lady Anne's staff, she should have informed me."

Pickett, painfully aware of having said precisely the wrong thing, hastened to reassure her. "I—I'm sure my lady is not displeased, precisely. Perhaps, being recently bereaved, she merely wishes for the comfort of a familiar face."

Mrs. Holland raised a skeptical eyebrow. "And your face

alone of all her ladyship's acquaintance can provide her with this comfort?"

Pickett felt his face grow warm and, not for the first time, deplored his tendency to blush. "I should have said, rather, a familiar way of doing things." Seeing the housekeeper was not convinced, he added, "My presence here may well be unnecessary, ma'am, but surely one newly widowed, and under such circumstances, must be forgiven a few eccentricities."

If Mrs. Holland did not wholeheartedly embrace this suggestion, at least she did not dispute it. She stepped aside, albeit grudgingly, allowing Pickett to enter. "Do not think that you will be given special privileges merely because you are in the employ of a viscountess," Mrs. Holland cautioned. "While you are here, you will be expected to follow the same rules as the rest of the staff."

"Yes, ma'am," murmured Pickett, wishing only that he might be allowed to put down a valise which was by this time growing quite heavy.

"You will rise each morning at six o'clock," the housekeeper continued, progressing through the servants' hall at a stately pace which, though undoubtedly befitting her dignity, did nothing to alleviate Pickett's burden. "Breakfast for the staff is served promptly at seven. Punctuality is imperative—any servant not appearing at the breakfast table will be obliged to wait until the noon meal for nourishment. Dinner is at one, and supper at half past eight. Like Lady Anne's own footmen, you will be allotted two pints of beer a day to drink with meals, but drunkenness will not be tolerated. You will also be required to wear livery and hair powder while on duty."

"Yes, ma'am," said Pickett again, mentally ticking off these instructions on fingers that were beginning to feel as if they were permanently curved around the handle of his valise.

"Like all the other footmen, you will of course be under the direct supervision of Mr. Smithers, the butler, but I do not think I overstep my authority when I tell you that slipping out to the tavern after the family retires is strictly forbidden, as is any form of dalliance with the female staff. And now," she added, glancing at the longcase clock against the adjacent wall, "you may have half an hour to unpack your belongings and make yourself presentable before assisting in the preparations for dinner."

"But—her ladyship—"

"Lady Fieldhurst can have no immediate need of you, since she has gone to the village. She will, of course, be informed of your arrival upon her return."

With this Pickett had to be content. Still, he felt a pang of disappointment. She had been in the village all along, and he had missed her.

"And now, since Molly has nothing better to do with herself, she may show you to your room—after which," added Mrs. Holland, fixing the maid with a gimlet eye, "she will return promptly to me for further instructions."

Molly, all eagerness to perform this task, lifted her skirts a bit higher than was strictly necessary and preceded Pickett up the back stairs, rounded hips swaying provocatively as she mounted each riser. "You'll have a room all to yourself since James—he's second footman, and it's his room you'll be sleeping in—had to go see about his mum, soon as the bridge was fixed."

Pickett was well acquainted with the bridge, since it—or rather, its absence—had figured prominently in Lady Fieldhurst's letter. "Had a lot of rain lately, have you?"

"Lud, you don't know the half of it! The river flooding its banks, the bridge washing right out, the vicarage burning to the ground with the poor old vicar inside—I'll never forget that night if I live to be a hundred, so help me!"

Pickett would have pressed for more information, but at that moment she reached the top of the stairs and turned back to face him—an action which, intentional or no, placed her substantial bosom scant inches from the end of his nose. Pickett dropped back to the next lowest step in order to avoid a far more intimate acquaintance with Molly than he had any desire for.

"All the men servants have their quarters in this wing," she explained, gesturing toward a shadowy expanse of uncarpeted corridor. To Pickett's immense relief, she turned her back on him and set off down the hallway, pointing out the various rooms as they passed.

"First door on the left is Charles, the under butler. Then Ned—he's first footman—then Robert, what valets for Master Philip whenever he's home from school. James has the room on the end, a little apart from the rest on account of him snoring."

Pickett wondered at her knowledge of the sleeping habits of the male staff, but judged it best not to inquire too closely. Halfway down the corridor, she stopped at the door of a tiny chamber which made his two hired rooms above a Drury Lane chandler's shop seem palatial by comparison. Though spartanly furnished with no more than a single narrow bed, a scarred wardrobe, a three-legged stool, and a rickety washstand bearing an earthenware pitcher, so small was the room that even these meager furnishings rendered it cramped. Still, it was meticulously clean—the credit for which condition, he suspected, must go to Mrs. Holland's iron-fisted management of her staff—and well lit with sunlight from a single window. He crossed the floor to this aperture, twitched back the single threadbare linen panel that served as a curtain, and looked out over a straight drop to a flagstone terrace fifty feet below.

He frowned. There was no conveniently placed tree or downspout, nor any other object which might assist him in making a nocturnal descent from the window, should the need arise. In fact, the nearest structure appeared to be the stables, situated some two hundred yards away. This was hardly the ideal situation from which to conduct a clandestine investigation; should he wish to examine the vicarage (or, indeed, anything else), he would be obliged to navigate the corridor, the back stair, and the servants' hall—this last under the disapproving eye of Mrs. Holland.

He cast another longing glance at the stables. Why hadn't he thought to pose as Lady Fieldhurst's groom instead? But even as his mind raised the question, he knew the answer. Aside from the fact that he had a very limited acquaintance with horses, a groom's access to her ladyship would be far more restricted than a footman's. No, he decided, allowing the curtain to fall back into place, whatever the disadvantages, he was better off here than in the stables.

He turned away from the window and received a shock that almost sent him running for the stables, their shortcomings notwithstanding. Molly bent over his narrow bed, plumping his pillow invitingly and at the same time affording him an uninterrupted view of her considerable cleavage.

"Anything else I can do for you, ducky?"

Pickett had no great faith in his ability to powder his hair unassisted, but the predatory gleam in Molly's eye gave him to understand that she was far more interested in taking things off than putting them on.

"N-no, thank you, I wouldn't want to get you in trouble—" He blushed at the unintended implications of this speech. "That is, Mrs. Holland will likely be expecting you—"

Molly gave a disdainful sniff. "Mrs. Holland, my eye! If there was ever a Mr. Holland, I've never seen hair nor hide of him! The old battle-axe expects us all to act as if we was as dried up and spinsterish as she is."

Still, Pickett's warning had apparently served its purpose.

Molly made no further advances, but gave the mattress one last pat and betook herself from the room. Pickett waited until he heard her footsteps clattering down the stairs, then closed his door, removed Thomas's livery from his valise, and set about the alterations that would transform him from a reasonably independent Bow Street operative to a lackey at the housekeeper's beck and call. If his hands trembled slightly during the application of the dreaded hair powder, it was very likely due to the fact that he found himself in the uncomfortable position of maintaining an incognito in the presence of no less than two disconcerting females—one of whom disliked him on sight for reasons he could not fathom, the other who appeared to like him a great deal too much for his peace of mind. Certainly his nervous state could have nothing at all to do with the fact that he would very shortly be coming face-to-face with the woman who had haunted his dreams for the last two months.

Lady Fieldhurst formed the habit of making daily treks to the village a full three days before Pickett might reasonably be expected to arrive. She always contrived to time her arrival so that she might be partaking of tea or lemonade at the Pig and Whistle just as the stage arrived from Leeds, and she always sat at a table near the window overlooking the courtyard, from which vantage point she might observe the passengers as they disembarked. But although she scanned each day's new arrivals for some sign of a tall young man with curling dark hair tied with a ribbon at the nape of his neck, no such individual materialized out of the crowd of weary, cranky travelers collecting their belongings from the boot and booking rooms for the night.

After the fifth day's repetition of this fruitless errand, the viscountess was beginning to feel the strain. As she gazed out the window to the bustling stable yard below, she sipped her tepid tea and entertained a series of increasingly melancholy thoughts. Had her letter somehow gone astray in the post and never reached its intended destination? Worse, had Mr. Pickett met with an accident somewhere along the route north? Perhaps he was not coming at all; perhaps he considered her an hysterical female who, having had one encounter with violent death, now read foul play into every tragic accident. For some reason this possibility seemed more galling than all the rest.

She looked away from the window long enough to refresh her teacup from the steaming pot, and was disconcerted to see the deceased vicar himself entering the hostelry. But no, a closer look revealed a man who, although close to late Mr. Danvers in age, bore no real resemblance to him. What, then, could have given her such a bizarre impression? Surely it had more to do with the man's costume than any physical similarity; like Mr. Danvers, he was dressed in the well-cut yet sober attire of the country cleric. As Lady Fieldhurst watched, he approached the proprietor and requested a room.

"Aye, sir, and how many nights will you be staying?" inquired this worthy.

"Only the one," said the new arrival. "I'll be conducting the funeral service for poor Mr. Danvers upon the morrow. After that, I shall be returning to my own parish."

The innkeeper blinked at him in some consternation. "I'm afraid you'll have to cool your heels a bit, Reverend. We've had too much rain to be burying. Ground's too soggy by half."

"Dear me!" exclaimed the parson. "What has been done with the—where is—?"

"The body's laid out all right and tight in the church vestry. I expect we'll have him safely underground by the end of the week, if the weather holds."

"Oh dear, oh dear," fretted the vicar. "When I agreed to read the burial service, I didn't anticipate being away from my own flock for so long."

"Meaning no disrespect, parson, but couldn't the curate do the burial just as well? He's a good lad, and that much like a son to poor old Mr. Danvers—him having no family of his own, leastways none that I ever heard of."

Lady Fieldhurst, her attention now fully engaged, silently shooed away the serving wench offering a plate of bread and butter, and bent her ear to the conversation still in progress.

"No doubt it was because of Mr. Meriwether's attachment to Mr. Danvers that Sir Gerald hoped to spare him the pain of conducting the burial," suggested the cleric. "Whatever the reason, Sir Gerald, who has the living in his gift, took it upon himself to make the arrangements—Mr. Danvers, as you say, having no family of his own."

"Aye, he's a good man, the baronet—always done right by his tenants."

"And, having given him my word, I shall stay long enough to honor it and trust that my own curate will tend the flock until I return."

With many assurances that the funeral could very likely be held by the end of the week, the innkeeper ushered his guest upstairs to his room. The conversation was quickly drowned in the clatter of boots on uncarpeted steps, but Lady Fieldhurst had much to consider nonetheless. If Mr. Pickett failed to arrive before the end of the week, his ability to investigate would be severely diminished. The vicar himself would be laid to rest in the churchyard, and Sir Gerald would eventually grant the living to a new vicar, who would no doubt wish the ruins of the old vicarage cleared away and construction of a new one begun. If Mr. Pickett delayed much longer, he would find very little evidence left to examine.

She glanced out the window once more. The stage had long since departed for its next stop, and the stable yard was now vacant but for a chambermaid beating a rug, a groom smoking a pipe, and two dogs dozing in the late afternoon sun. With a silent plea for Mr. Pickett to make haste, she pushed her empty teacup aside and abandoned her vigil for yet another day.

She arrived back at Hollingshead Place just in time to dress for dinner. After exchanging her gray walking dress and muddy half boots for the striped silk she had worn on the night of the fire, she rang for Rose to dress her hair.

"Oh!" she cried when that overzealous abigail drew the brush through her curls with more force than was strictly necessary. "Why not pull out a handful, while you are about it?"

"Oh, my! I'm ever so sorry, my lady," said Rose, her guilty, frightened gaze meeting the viscountess's in the mirror. "I didn't mean to be so rough, 'pon my word!"

Lady Fieldhurst, seeing the girl's eyes rapidly filling with tears, heaved a sigh. "It is I who should beg your pardon, for being so cross."

" 'Tis poor Mr. Danvers's death what's got everyone on edge, your ladyship," said the maid sympathetically. " 'Tis the same in the servants' hall."

Mistress and maid turned their mutual attention back to the task at hand, Lady Fieldhurst surrendering her head without further complaint, and Rose plying her brush more gently. At length, her ladyship's toilette was complete, and Rose was dismissed. She bobbed a curtsy and crossed the room to the service door, then turned back. "Oh, I almost forgot! Begging your pardon, my lady, but I was to tell you that your footman arrived from London today and will be waiting on you tonight at table."

"My footman?" echoed Lady Fieldhurst in some confusion, but Rose had already bobbed another curtsy and disappeared through the service door.

The viscountess went downstairs in some bewilderment. What

was Thomas doing here? It was possible, she supposed, that he had come north to convey Mr. Pickett's regrets, although why Bow Street should favor such an expensive and time-consuming means of communication quite escaped her.

A still greater surprise was in store. When the dinner gong sounded and she accepted Sir Gerald's escort to the dining room, she discovered that the footman who stood behind her chair was not Thomas at all, but a very tall young man in blue and silver Fieldhurst livery whose sleeves appeared to be about two inches too short. She blinked, mistrusting the evidence of her own eyes. Yes, his eyes were brown (as was his hair beneath its coating of white powder, she did not doubt) and the nose was slightly crooked, as if it had once been broken. He did not look at her, but stood rigidly erect at his post, staring straight ahead with the expressionless countenance of the well-trained servant. Indeed, he showed no signs of recognizing her at all until she had taken her seat and was in the act of spreading her napkin on her lap. When it slipped from her trembling fingers and fluttered to the floor, he was at her side in an instant. He stooped to retrieve the large square of linen, and when she glanced up at him, she was almost certain he winked.

The dinner that followed ranked among the longest meals of her life. Somehow she managed to resist the urge to stare at him over her shoulder; after all, one should take no more notice of one's servants than one would of the furniture. To wheel about in one's chair to address the footman would be completely outside the pale. Still, she was all too aware of his presence at her back, and of his white-gloved hands refilling her wineglass. It was with an effort that she dragged her attention back to the conversation at the table and found Sir Gerald posing a question.

"Did you find anything in our humble village to interest you, my Lady Fieldhurst?"

"Yes, Sir Gerald, as a matter of fact, I did." The viscountess plunged eagerly into speech, lest the family notice her distraction. "The vicar of a neighboring parish arrived today to conduct the burial service for Mr. Danvers. I understand you made the arrangements yourself, as Mr. Danvers had no family. I find that very thoughtful of you."

"Nonsense!" declared Sir Gerald, looking pleased nonetheless. "Least a fellow can do, under the circumstances. And then there's my duty to my position—*noblesse oblige* and all that, you know. You'll learn all about that someday, my lad," he added as an aside to his son.

Philip muttered something unintelligible which gave the company to understand that he was not looking forward to assuming the mantle of his father's responsibilities. Sir Gerald glowered at the boy, and Lady Fieldhurst judged it time to intervene.

"The general consensus in the village seems to be that the funeral may be held before the end of the week, assuming the weather holds," she observed.

"Aye, and I for one will be glad to have it over. The sooner everything gets back to normal, the better off we'll all be."

"But what of the vacant benefice, Papa?" asked Miss Hollingshead. "Will you grant the living to our cousin Mr. Meriwether?"

"Harrumph!" Sir Gerald cleared his throat noisily. "No sense in rushing into things, I always say."

His wife concurred. "It is unseemly, Emma, to speculate on such things when poor Mr. Danvers has not yet been laid to rest. I am sure when the time comes your father will make the best decision for all concerned."

Emma Hollingshead wilted under this mild rebuke, and the conversation thereafter grew more general and considerably less interesting. At last Lady Anne rose, and Lady Fieldhurst seized the opportunity to make good her escape.

"My head aches most vilely," she declared, pressing one black-gloved hand to her temple. "If you will excuse me, Lady Anne, Miss Hollingshead, I shall seek my bed."

"By all means," said her hostess. "I thought during dinner that you did not look at all the thing. Depend upon it, it is all this walking to the village. A little such exercise is all very well, but you will wear yourself to the bone if you go on in this way."

Lady Fieldhurst agreed readily, having previously given no thought to how she might abandon, now that it was no longer needed, the habit she had so firmly established.

She climbed the curving staircase to the accompaniment of the ladies' best wishes for her improved health, forcing her steps to remain slow and steady until she reached the floor above, well out of sight of anyone in the hall below. Then she picked up her gray silk skirts and hurried the last few feet down the corridor to her assigned bedchamber, where she shut herself in, turned the key in the lock, and tugged vigorously on the bell-pull. She had not long to wait, but to Lady Fieldhurst, pacing the carpet, every moment seemed an eternity until at last she heard a faint tap on the service door. To her relief, it opened to reveal not Rose bearing a freshly laundered nightrail (or, worse, a vile-tasting concoction for her nonexistent headache), but her counterfeit footman bearing a scuttle filled with coal.

"You rang, my lady?" he asked with a formality belied by the twinkle in his eyes. While she struggled for words, he stepped past her and knelt before the fireplace, where he emptied his scuttle into the grate.

"What is that?" she asked, momentarily distracted.

"Coals for your fire. Mrs. Holland is already inclined to distrust me, and since she rules the servants' hall with a rod of iron, I thought it best to provide myself with an errand."

"But why should you care for Mrs. Holland's good opinion,

and what are you doing in the servants' hall, and in such a guise?"

Having finished his task, he rose and brushed the knees of his blue satin breeches. "I'm pleased to see you again, too, my lady."

His tone, deceptively meek, startled a laugh out of her ladyship. "And now you must think me shockingly rag-mannered! Of course I am pleased to see you—heaven knows I have thought of little else for the past se'ennight!—but I never expected to see you like *this!*" The wave of her hand encompassed every part of his disguise, from his powdered hair to his white silk stockings.

I have thought of little else for the past se'ennight . . . It would be the height of folly, Pickett knew, to refine too much upon those words. On the night they had met, Lady Fieldhurst would have taken a lover, one Lord Rupert Latham, had not the discovery of her husband's body interrupted their assignation. Pickett had little doubt that, with that particular impediment removed, Lord Rupert had lost no time in worming his way back into her ladyship's good graces, as well as her bed. Wrenching his mind away from a picture too revolting to contemplate, he concentrated instead on the lady as she stood before him now, taking in the subtle changes wrought over the last two months.

"If I may say so without seeming impertinent, my lady, you're looking very well," he said, gesturing toward her elegant gray gown. "I see you've put off your blacks."

"I have gone into half-mourning," she admitted. "A bit premature, I admit, but it seemed—hypocritical—to do otherwise."

Pickett could see how it might be a bit awkward, mourning one man while sleeping with another. "And—and how fares his lordship?"

The look she gave him was one of utter bewilderment. "His

lordship is dead—as you, of all people, have reason to know."

"I-I meant Lord Rupert."

"Oh! Yes, of-of course. Lord Rupert," Lady Fieldhurst stammered, not quite certain why the mention of the man who had almost been her lover should render her tongue-tied. "I-I suppose he is well enough, at least I have heard nothing to the contrary. In fact, I have not seen him since the trial."

"Oh!" said Pickett, suddenly feeling much lighter at heart.

"But how came you by the Fieldhurst livery, and to what purpose?"

"I borrowed it from Thomas. I hope you don't mind."

"If Thomas did not object, I can hardly complain," observed the viscountess. "But *why?*"

"You asked me to keep my association with Bow Street secret," he reminded her. "I can learn much more here, living in the servants' quarters, gossiping with the staff, than ever I could staying at the Pig and Whistle."

"I hadn't thought of that." She arched a quizzical eyebrow. "Did you, by any chance, offer any explanation as to why Lady Anne's servants were insufficient to my needs?"

"I told Mrs. Holland within earshot of the kitchen maid that you'd grown a bit eccentric since your husband's death. I daresay the whole household knows by this time."

"I might have known!" declared her ladyship with a sigh of resignation. "You are nothing if not resourceful, Mr. Pickett."

"Thank you, my lady. I shall do my best not to disappoint. In the meantime, though, if I am to be your footman, I must point out that you do not call Thomas by his surname."

"It would be highly improper of me to call you by your given name!"

"It would be highly improper of you to call your footman anything else."

She threw up her black-gloved hands in surrender. "Very

well, when we are in company, I shall address you by your Christian name. But when we are alone, it is only fitting that I call you Mr. Pickett."

"And risk forgetting, or being overheard? No, I think I had best be 'John' for the duration."

"You drive a hard bargain," conceded Lady Fieldhurst, then added with a twinkle in her eye, "but you should be aware that it is not at all the thing for a servant to correct his mistress."

"Beg pardon, my lady," said Pickett, bowing deeply from the waist. "I shall bear it in mind."

Her smile warmed him all the way down to his toes. "Oh, I'm so glad you have come! It has been perfectly dreadful, not being able to confide my fears to anyone, while as for the atmosphere in this house, it is thick with rumor and suspicion."

"You believe someone in the house set the fire that killed the vicar?"

"I think it must have been." She crossed the room to take a seat in the chair before the fireplace. "But I must not keep you standing here! Do sit down."

"I've been sitting in a crowded stage coach for the past three days," he reminded her, but took a seat at the writing desk nonetheless. "Now, exactly what is it that you suspect?"

"I think—I think perhaps Mr. Danvers did not burn to death in the fire."

"I saw the vicarage on my way up from the village," Pickett reminded her. "I doubt any man could survive such an inferno."

"No, but—you may think it foolish of me, but I find myself wondering if perhaps he was already dead."

Pickett's eyebrows rose. "And the house burned after the fact to destroy any evidence? Tell me, my lady, what makes you suspect such a thing?"

"I returned to my room shortly after dinner, and had opened the window to see if the storm had passed when I heard a noise—a sharp, cracking sound. I thought at the time that lightning must have struck a tree somewhere in the Home Wood, but now I think—no, I am almost certain it was a gunshot."

"I believe the two can sound amazingly alike, my lady."

Lady Fieldhurst bristled. "Pray do not patronize me! You forget, I am country bred, the daughter of an avid sportsman. I know what a firearm sounds like."

"I beg your pardon, my lady. I meant no disrespect."

Deflated, Lady Fieldhurst dashed a hand wearily over her eyes. "No, it is I who should beg your pardon. I did not urge you to come all the way from London only so that I might snap at you. In fact, my nerves are shockingly on edge."

"It would be more shocking if they were not, given that you suspect you may be dwelling under the same roof with a murderer."

"The murderer—if murderer there be—may not be in the house at this moment, but I think he must certainly have been on the night of the fire. The bridge washed out while we were at dinner, you see. The vicarage was completely cut off from everything except the church and Hollingshead Place. Oh, and its Home Wood. There are gypsies camped there. Do they count?"

"We won't rule them out just yet," said Pickett, withdrawing a small notebook from the inside pocket of his blue and silver coat. "Now, who was present at this dinner?"

"The Hollingsheads, of course—Sir Gerald, Lady Anne, their son Philip, and their daughter Emma," she said, ticking them off on her fingers. "Their younger daughter, Susannah, had come down from the schoolroom for the occasion, along with her governess, Miss Grantham. Then there was poor Mr. Danvers and his curate, Mr. Meriwether. And Mr. Carrington. I didn't speak with him much, but I had the impression he was something of a nabob."

"A nabob?" echoed Pickett, pencil poised in midair.

"One who has made a fortune in the East—tea, perhaps, or something similar. Then there were Lord and Lady Kendall, along with their son, the Honourable Robert Kendall. They are near neighbors of the Hollingsheads. Lord Kendall is a Justice of the Peace."

Pickett grimaced. "Please, tell me Lord Kendall didn't do it!"

"Why not?"

"Because," he explained, "as a Justice of the Peace, he is the one I would apply to for an arrest warrant."

"Oh, dear! Yes, I can see how that would be a bit awkward for you."

"Did any of them appear to have a grudge against the vicar? Might anyone expect to profit from his death?"

"Well, none of them would have to listen to him talk about that book of his, but I doubt that constitutes a motive for murder."

Pickett looked up from his scribbling to ask, "What book?"

"Mr. Danvers was writing a voluminous tome chronicling the history of the village church," she explained. "He apparently delighted in sharing tidbits from his research, often and at great length, whether his audience wished to hear them or not."

"And so someone killed the old boy in self-defense, before he bored them all to death?" concluded Pickett with a hint of a smile.

"Pray do not joke about it!" Lady Fieldhurst beseeched him, shuddering. "It may sound absurd, but it was altogether ghastly."

"I beg your pardon. It must have been most uncomfortable for you."

"Not half so uncomfortable for me as it was for poor Mr. Danvers."

"Indeed. Was there anyone else who might stand to gain if the vicar were out of the way?"

The viscountess frowned at the memory of a certain overheard conversation. "Out of the way. It is interesting that you should put it that way."

"What are you thinking?"

Lady Fieldhurst rose from her chair and began to pace the thickly carpeted floor. "I was thinking of the curate, Mr. Meriwether. He is in love with Emma Hollingshead, but her parents disapprove, at least in part because of his lack of fortune. Now that the vicar is dead, Mr. Meriwether may well be granted the living which would allow him to marry Miss Hollingshead. But it hardly seems a wealthy enough position to kill for."

"I've known men to be murdered for much less," Pickett observed.

"But I doubt Mr. Meriwether would win Lady Anne's approval in any case. Apparently he is a distant relation, and Lady Anne remarked within my hearing that he was illegitimate, or nearly so." She pondered the implications of her ladyship's words. "How can one be nearly illegitimate?"

Beneath his head of white powder, Pickett flushed crimson. "Perhaps Mr. and Mrs. Meriwether were blessed with a son rather less than nine months after the wedding," he suggested.

"Oh! I daresay you are right. Certainly Lady Anne would not wish her daughter to marry where there had been any hint of scandal. She has very high expectations for Miss Hollingshead."

"On the other hand, what better way to eliminate an unwanted suitor than to see him hanged for murder?"

Lady Fieldhurst wheeled about to look at him in surprise. "I beg your pardon?"

"Miss Hollingshead and Mr. Meriwether plan to marry as soon as he is granted the living. Lady Anne—or Sir Gerald, if you prefer, or the two of them together—are not delighted with the match, but they know any attempt to break up the lovers will only strengthen their attachment. So they kill the vicar, and

Mr. Meriwether, who has the most obvious—indeed, at this point the *only*—motive is convicted of the crime. Mr. Meriwether goes to the gallows, and the heartbroken Miss Hollingshead no longer has the will to resist her parents' plans for her."

"That is a perfectly horrid scenario, Mr. Pickett!"

"John," he corrected her. "And you are right: it is perfectly horrid. It is also pure speculation at this point. We don't even know for certain that there was a murder at all."

She stopped before the fireplace and gazed down into the flames. "Was it wrong of me to send for you on nothing more than a foolish whim?"

Pickett rose and crossed the room to stand beside her. "No, my lady, it was not wrong."

"The coroner seemed quite convinced the vicar was burned to death when the vicarage was struck by lightning."

"In that case, I don't think much of the coroner. I think it highly unlikely that the vicarage was ever struck by lightning."

"Indeed? What makes you say so?"

"Simple probability. Lightning tends to strike objects that are higher than their surroundings—a tall building, or a tree near an open field. The bell tower of the church would have been a much more attractive target—so would Hollingshead Place, for that matter, standing as it does on higher ground."

The viscountess blinked at this revelation. "I, for one, am very glad it did not! I can just imagine the chaos if the entire household had been obliged to evacuate in the middle of dinner."

"Exactly so. Which brings us to the next question: why did Mr. Danvers apparently make no attempt to escape from the burning building? Was he in any way infirm?"

"Why no, not that I could tell. He was not a young man—I daresay he was sixty years old, at the least reckoning—but he was quite spry. In fact, he would have traveled uphill to Hollingshead Place on foot, had Mr. Carrington not offered him a ride in his own carriage, and he insisted upon walking back to the vicarage in spite of Sir Gerald's best efforts to persuade him otherwise."

"Did he show any signs of deafness—using an ear trumpet, or perhaps talking a bit too loudly?"

She shook her head. "If you are thinking he might have slept through the storm and awakened only after the house was ablaze, I fear that theory won't wash. According to Lord Kendall, his body was discovered in the part of the house that was once the study. He had apparently not yet retired for the night."

Pickett drummed his gloved fingers soundlessly on the mantel. "Hmm. He was already on the ground floor, yet evidently made no effort to leave the house. We must assume, then, that someone or something prevented him." He cocked his head and regarded her thoughtfully. "Tell me, has he been buried yet?"

"No. The ground is too saturated from the rain. His body has been laid out, though, and the coffin is being kept in the church."

Pickett nodded. "Appropriate enough."

"And cool and dark, which is more to the purpose." Her eyes widened as a singularly gruesome thought occurred to her. "You don't intend to prize the lid!"

"Probably. I'll want a closer look at the ruins, too. They may still be smoldering, but they should have cooled off enough for me to poke around a bit."

"Really, John," said her ladyship, blushing a little at the unaccustomed intimacy of using his given name, "what kind of servant demands time off after less than twenty-four hours on the job? I cannot be optimistic about your future in domestic service."

Chapter 4

John Pickett Belowstairs

Pickett arose at dawn the following morning, breathing a silent thanks to the mother of the absent footman, James, for requiring her son's presence at such an opportune time; he had no desire for a witness to his early morning wanderings. He donned not his borrowed livery, but his own brown serge coat, and crept from the room carrying his shoes in his hand. He made his way down the corridor past the other footmen's chambers, freezing in his tracks when a growling noise issued from behind the door to his left. He let out a ragged breath; apparently James was not the only one of the footmen who snored.

Having successfully navigated the first stage of his escape, he started stealthily down the stairs. He had a bad moment when the third tread from the top creaked beneath his weight, but although he paused for a moment to listen, no angry voice challenged his presence. He resolved to avoid that particular step in the future, and continued his journey. As he crossed the shadowy kitchen, he wondered fleetingly which female he most wished to avoid: the censorious Mrs. Holland, or the concupiscent Molly.

He received his answer as he drew abreast of the door to the wine cellar, and heard the housekeeper's voice issuing from within.

"—Surely mistaken, Mr. Smithers. You must have miscounted."

"I assure you, madam, I took a thorough inventory just last

week when I prepared an order for Berry Brothers," the butler answered. "A bottle of the eighty-six Hermitage is unquestionably missing, along with two bottles of the ninety-four Sauternes. Much as it pains me to cast aspersions onto anyone's morals, I must ask: have you noticed any erratic behavior on the part of any servant which might suggest a weakness for strong drink?"

"Hmm . . ." The housekeeper pondered the question. "It seems queer to me that several bottles of wine should turn up missing very shortly after the arrival of that fellow from London."

"Lady Fieldhurst's footman?"

"The very same. He seems to me a shifty sort who would like nothing better than to get up the skirts of the female staff. If he thought to loosen them up a bit with a glass or two from the master's cellar, well, I wouldn't put it past him."

Pickett blinked at this hitherto unsuspected facet of his character. What would Mrs. Holland say if she knew that, far from being the seducer of innocents she took him for, he was the innocent, at least in the sexual sense? Not that he hadn't had his share of opportunities; aside from the predatory Molly, there was always Lucy, who considered it her mission in life to deprive him of his virtue. Although Molly scared him to death, he might have been tempted to oblige Lucy, had he not seen enough of disease, poverty, and prostitution to make him resolve to save himself for the woman who would one day be his wife—a hypothetical female who had recently acquired a marked resemblance to the lady sleeping upstairs in the best guest chamber.

He reminded himself that it was this lady, not Mrs. Holland, toward whom his duty lay. Still clutching his shoes, he stole past the wine cellar and soon made his escape from the house. He paused on the back stoop long enough to slip on his shoes, then set out down the hill toward the ruined shell where Mr. Danvers had met his death.

The distance from Hollingshead Place to the burned-out vicarage was not great, but to Pickett, a Londoner born and bred, and accustomed to the anonymity inherent in sharing one's habitat with more than a million of his fellow men, the long expanse of unbroken green sloping downward toward the road seemed almost nakedly exposed. Anyone glancing out the window might see Lady Fieldhurst's footman stealing furtively toward the scene of the recent conflagration. Then again, Pickett reasoned, surely such inquisitive behavior could not be considered unreasonable for a newcomer to the vicinity, particularly one possessed of a lively curiosity. If confronted, Pickett decided, he would feign a morbid fascination with the macabre. Surely such a pretense would not prove to be beyond his capabilities; his landlady, Mrs. Catchpole, frequently accused him of just such a peculiarity, usually just before urging him to find himself a new profession and a wife. Such a proclivity might prove useful, should he be forced into an encounter with Mrs. Holland before having an opportunity to change his clothes and wash the smell of smoke from his person. He hoped matters would not come to such a pass; he suspected Mrs. Holland's cure for this idiosyncrasy would be even less welcome than Mrs. Catchpole's.

The stench of smoke, discernable even from Hollingshead Place, grew increasingly stronger until at last he reached the ruined vicarage. Its blackened stone walls seemed to be waiting for him, the gaping windows staring sightlessly like a dead man's eyes. The roof had burned away, leaving the charred interior open to the sky, but the early morning sun was as yet too low to provide much in the way of illumination. Within the stone walls, great scorched beams sagged at drunken angles, resembling nothing so much as an enormous game of jackstraws. Broken glass and charred debris crunched beneath Pickett's feet, and although the ruins no longer smoldered, a feeble curl of smoke occasionally rose from the ashes when prodded with the toe of his boot.

Pickett had been confident enough the previous evening, talking to the viscountess, but now, confronted with the magnitude of the destruction, he felt more than a little daunted by the task before him. He had been a Bow Street Runner for less than a twelvemonth, and it had never fallen to him to investigate any case involving fire. How did one gather evidence when all was reduced to ashes? He thought of Mr. Colquhoun and wished he had possessed the foresight to solicit the magistrate's advice. He still might do so, through the medium of the post. But he could not shake the conviction that any show of ineptitude on his part would result in his being recalled to Bow Street and the odious Foote dispatched to Yorkshire in his place. No, he would solve this crime (if, indeed, crime there were) on his own, or he would perish in the attempt.

With renewed determination, he ducked beneath a fallen beam—and found himself confronting a dark young man clad in rough homespun. For a long moment the two stared at one another in mutual astonishment. Then one of the tortured beams creaked, shattering the silence. Released from his spell, the intruder took to his heels, bounding across the blackened debris littering the floor and through the gaping doorway at the rear of the house.

"You, there! Halt!"

Pickett started at once in pursuit, but halfway across the ruined room, his toe struck something hard, and he fell forward with sufficient force to knock the breath from his body. He scrambled to his feet and covered the remaining distance to the door with as much speed as he could muster, knowing already what he would find. Leaning against the doorframe and gasping for breath, he surveyed his surroundings grimly. No sign of life stirred in the small garden at the rear of the house. The intruder, whoever he was, had no doubt sought refuge in the woods beyond.

Had Pickett been in London, he would not have hesitated to plunge forward in pursuit, for he knew Bow Street and its environs like the back of his hand. However, he could see nothing to be gained by getting himself lost in the woods, so he returned to the ruin to locate the object which had brought about his downfall. He found it after a brief search, a long, heavy object whose black color owed nothing to its recent trial by fire. Indeed, it had been crafted to withstand the flames, for it proved to be an iron poker. Pickett gauged the distance from the fireplace to the poker's current location in what appeared to be the center of the room and estimated it to be no less than eight, perhaps as much as ten feet.

He dropped the poker and picked his way to the fireplace for a closer look. The damage here was so extensive as to render most of the debris unidentifiable, but for the remains of what must have once been a handsome fowling piece mounted over the mantel. Its wooden stock had completely burned away, leaving only the barrel and firing mechanism. Pickett could not help thinking that, come autumn, the local grouse population would have little to fear from that particular weapon. Still, its existence was interesting in the light of Lady Fieldhurst's conviction that she had heard a gunshot. And yet, what kind of man—or woman, for that matter—would be so cold-blooded as to shoot a man to death and then coolly mount the murder weapon on the dead man's wall? No, it would appear that the vicar's mysterious death must have been no more than a tragic accident, the result of some flammable object exploding after being left too close to the fire.

Still, Pickett could not be entirely satisfied. What sort of explosion would hurl an iron poker ten feet across the room, yet leave the ash can undisturbed upon the hearth? He picked his way across the room to inspect a shard of broken glass from the shattered windowpanes, and squinted when bright sunlight hit him full in the face. The sun was riding higher in the sky now, peering over the window sill. Up the hill at Hollingshead Place, the family would soon be gathering for breakfast, and he would be expected to wait upon the viscountess. Somehow he must communicate to Lady Fieldhurst his need to have the afternoon free, for it was obvious that Mr. Danvers's eternal slumber must not be allowed to go undisturbed. Pickett only hoped the vicar's earthly remains would yield more information than his erstwhile residence had done. He tossed the shard of glass back onto the ruined floor, then made his way back up the hill to Hollingshead Place.

The cavernous kitchen was still dark, but a fire had been lit in the great stove for the day's cooking. Pickett wished he might linger in front of it long enough to ward off the morning chill, but the fire's very existence made it clear that the household was beginning to stir. He had best waste no time in returning to his own room. To this end, he crossed the kitchen and headed for the staircase at the end of the corridor. He was less than twenty feet from his goal when a door flew open on his left, making him start. There stood the ubiquitous Mrs. Holland with the butler at her elbow, apparently enjoying their morning coffee, judging from the twin curls of steam rising from the cups they held.

"You there!" barked the housekeeper. "What's-your-name!"

"Pickett, ma'am," he reminded her. "John Pickett."

"And what, pray, are you doing skulking about at such an hour?"

"Merely taking my morning constitutional," said Pickett, improvising rapidly. "In the city, it was always my habit—"

"You are not in the city any longer, John Pickett, so let us hear no more of it. Do you not agree, Mr. Smithers?"

The butler leaned closer, his nose twitching like a rabbit's. Pickett knew a moment's panic until he recalled the missing bottles of wine, and realized the man was trying to sniff his breath for any traces of alcohol. Apparently the butler was so intent upon finding evidence of liquor theft that he failed to notice the scent of smoke Pickett knew must cling to his hair and clothes.

"Indeed I do, Mrs. Holland." Mr. Smithers turned to address Pickett. "If you suffer from an excess of restless energy, young man, then after the family has breakfast you may assist Charles in washing and putting away the china, and Ned in polishing the silver. I am sure we can find more than enough activity to keep you occupied."

With these words, it seemed, battle was fairly joined. "I shall be happy to do so, Mr. Smithers," he said stiffly, "provided, of course, that my lady Fieldhurst has no need of me."

Having delivered as strong a parting shot as his present situation allowed, he turned and made his way up the stairs with as much dignity as he could muster. Alas, the morning quickly progressed from bad to worse. It soon became evident that he had grossly underestimated the time necessary for powdering his hair, and by the time he had completed this unfamiliar and messy exercise, the better part of the room looked as if it were the recipient of a freakish snowfall. Not wishing to be obliged to account to Mrs. Holland for this new infraction, he tidied up the worst of it before going down to breakfast—only to discover that the rest of the staff had already finished eating, and were in the process of clearing away the dishes.

"We missed you at breakfast, John," observed the housekeeper with a certain malicious satisfaction. "Perhaps by the time you join us for luncheon, you will have learned the importance of promptness."

"Yes, ma'am," he said meekly, and followed the other footmen to the breakfast room, where the family was shortly to gather for their own morning meal.

Lady Fieldhurst entered the breakfast room to find Sir Gerald fortifying himself with eggs, kippers, and steak while Lady Anne picked daintily at toast and marmalade. Susannah's absence was only to be expected—she would be partaking of breakfast in the schoolroom with her governess—but her brother Philip was there, looking very much the worse for wear with a pale face and bloodshot eyes. Of Emma Hollingshead there was no sign. Lady Fieldhurst murmured polite responses to her host and hostess's greetings, then crossed the room to the mahogany buffet where Pickett stood wearing his borrowed livery and a singularly wooden expression. It appeared that her own footman, Thomas, had taught him well, for surely no one watching him pour steaming coffee into her delicate Spode cup would have suspected that he was anything but a well-trained servant.

"Eggs, my lady?"

The viscountess searched this simple query for hidden meanings, and found none. "Thank you, John."

She allowed him to fill her plate with buttered eggs, toast, and marmalade, then joined Sir Gerald and Lady Anne at the table.

"Looks like the sun has finally decided to shine on us," Sir Gerald observed. "I'll wager you ladies will be glad enough to get out of the house for a change."

"Yes, indeed," agreed Lady Fieldhurst. "As lovely as your house is, I confess I am ready for a change of scenery. I thought I might go to the village today for some shopping."

"An excellent notion," applauded Lady Anne. "I regret that I cannot accompany you, as I must call on some of our tenants to see how they are faring after the recent storms. I've no doubt Emma would be pleased to take my place; in my experience, young girls are always eager to shop."

As if on cue, the door opened to admit Emma Hollingshead, fetchingly attired in a charming pink muslin gown which quite failed to disguise either her pallid complexion or the dark circles beneath her eyes.

"Ah, there you are, my dear," said Lady Anne, seemingly oblivious to her daughter's poor looks. "You would not object to accompanying Lady Fieldhurst on a shopping trip to the village, would you?"

"I should be pleased to do so," Miss Hollingshead said somewhat mechanically.

As this was not at all what Lady Fieldhurst had in mind, she was relieved to see that her proposed companion had no more liking for the scheme than she did herself. "Pray do not inconvenience yourself on my account, Miss Hollingshead," she beseeched the younger lady. "As my shopping these days is limited to blacks and grays, I fear you would find little enough pleasure in it."

"At least let me offer you the use of our carriage," Lady Anne persisted. "Our coachman, Gunning, will take you anywhere you may wish to go."

"You are too kind, my lady, but in truth, I would prefer to walk. The exercise will do me good. I shall take John along to carry my parcels."

The furtive smile she cast in Pickett's direction held more than a hint of mischief, and he found himself wondering just how many parcels he would be obliged to haul back up the hill.

"While I am out, I should like to stop by the church and see the Norman bell tower," the viscountess continued. "Mr. Danvers urged me to do so, and now I feel quite ashamed of myself for having put him off. I shall visit it today in honor of his memory."

"Hmph!" grunted Sir Gerald. "Can't imagine anyone but Danvers being interested in the thing. Daresay he went on about it for at least a chapter or two in that deuced boring book of his."

Lady Anne pointedly cleared her throat. "Gerald, my dear—"

"Yes, yes, I know: *'de mortuis nil nisi bonum,'* and all that. But if a fellow was a bore while he was alive, I don't see what good it does to pretend he wasn't, once he's dead."

"Perhaps Mr. Meriwether would consent to show you about the churchyard," suggested Lady Anne. "I could send him a note, if you wish."

"That will not be at all necessary," Lady Fieldhurst protested quickly. "I have no idea how long I might remain in the village, and I should hate for Mr. Meriwether to be kept kicking his heels at the church all day awaiting my arrival."

In truth, her concern was less for the curate's convenience than for the possibility that Emma Hollingshead might change her mind and decide to accompany her in the hopes of seeing her lover. But Miss Hollingshead's attention remained fixed upon the chocolate cooling in her cup. Still, Lady Fieldhurst decided to make good her escape before some other companion—Miss Susannah, perhaps, or her governess—was foisted upon her.

"I believe I shall go at once, before the sun grows uncomfortably warm. John," she added as an aside to Pickett, "allow me a moment to collect my bonnet, then meet me in the foyer."

When the viscountess descended the curving staircase to the foyer some five minutes later, John Pickett, that good and faithful servant, was awaiting her there. She acknowledged him with a nod, and although he selfishly wished for some more intimate communication, he could not but be grateful for her discretion. She paused before a large gilt-framed mirror long enough to tie the black ribbons of her plaited straw bonnet, and then the pair set out on foot, the viscountess leading the way while her *faux* footman followed several paces behind. Any umbrage Pickett might have been inclined to take at the lowliness of his present situation was considerably assuaged by the excellent view it afforded of Lady Fieldhurst's gently swaying hips. Once out of view of the house, however, she hung back long enough for him to catch up with her, then fell into step beside him.

"At last!" she declared fervently. "I thought breakfast would never end! Did you ever see two such gloomy pusses as Miss Hollingshead and her brother? And their parents' determination to pretend everything is normal somehow makes it even worse. I vow, staying in that house is enough to give anyone a fit of the dismals!"

"I can understand Miss Hollingshead's concern for her lover, but what of the boy? Was he fond of Mr. Danvers?"

Lady Fieldhurst recounted their brief exchange at the dinner table. "No, I should say Philip Hollingshead resented him. I believe Philip finds the country tedious, and has been amusing himself in ways his mama would not approve. I received the distinct impression that he has been stealing out of the house to attend cockfights, and that Mr. Danvers had found out, and informed his parents."

"Hmm," said Pickett, thinking of the missing wine bottles. "I wonder if that's not the only thing he's been stealing."

"But tell me, what did you find at the vicarage?"

"How did you know I've already been?" he asked in some surprise.

"There was a faint smell of smoke about the buffet this morning. No, no, you need not worry," she added hastily, seeing his puzzled expression turn to one of chagrin. "I had the advantage of knowing that you planned to pay a visit there. I doubt anyone else would have noticed."

"Particularly if they were looking for the smell of alcohol instead."

"I beg your pardon?" asked Lady Fieldhurst, bewildered.

Pickett shook his head. "Never mind."

"You must have been out and about very early, to be back in time for breakfast."

In fact, he had *not* been back in time for breakfast, at least not his own, but he saw no reason to burden the viscountess with this information. "Just after dawn, in fact."

Now it was Lady Fieldhurst's turn to feel chagrin. "Why so early? Surely you did not think I was serious when I chided you for wanting the afternoon free?"

Pickett regarded her with limpid brown eyes. "I dared not take the chance, my lady. A servant's life is a hard one, particularly with such an exacting taskmistress as mine."

She gave a startled laugh. "Very well, Mr. Pickett—John—I suppose I deserved that, after dragging you all the way from London on what might well prove to be a search for mares' nests."

"Not at all. In fact, I wanted to allow myself sufficient time to powder my hair. Besides being messy, the stuff makes me sneeze."

"I confess, I am not at all sorry to have been born too late for that particular fashion—"

She broke off in some confusion as Pickett left the road for the path leading to the church door.

"John?" After the initial awkwardness, she found it all too easy to call him by his Christian name. "Where are you going?"

"I beg your pardon," he said. "When you mentioned stopping by the church, I assumed the trip to the village was a ruse for my benefit."

"And so it is, for the most part. But we must go to the village first."

"Oh?" He returned to the road, and they set out in the direction of the village once more. "Why is that?"

"My dear John, it would be very odd for a lady to go shopping and not make a single purchase!"

"You would know best about that," he acknowledged, bowing to her superior wisdom.

"But now that we are alone, you must tell me: what did you find at the vicarage?"

"Nothing conclusive, I'm afraid."

"I feared as much."

He regarded her quizzically. "Was I so obvious?"

"Not to anyone else. But I know from experience that you get a certain light in your eyes when you are on the verge of making a discovery. When I saw you at breakfast, I knew that only a man whose efforts were unproductive could assume so wooden an expression."

"Hmm," said Pickett, pondering this statement, "I wonder if I have just been offered a compliment, or an insult?"

"Oh, a compliment, I assure you! I daresay it was a good thing for the sake of your incognito that you found nothing, for otherwise your expression must surely have given you away."

The ground grew softer as they approached the temporary bridge, and Pickett took her ladyship's arm to assist her across a muddy patch. When she tucked her hand into the crook of his elbow, Pickett's cup overflowed. Granted, it seemed a bit macabre to woo his lady while discussing a corpse, but then (as he was sure Mr. Colquhoun would not have hesitated to point out, had he been present), she was not his lady, and there could be no wooing on his part, macabre or otherwise.

And then, without warning, Pickett's belly betrayed him by loudly protesting his neglect.

Lady Fieldhurst regarded him quizzically. "You must have breakfasted very early indeed, if you are already impatient for luncheon."

"I haven't had anything to eat," Pickett confessed. "The despised hair powder took longer than expected, with the result that I missed eating the morning meal with the rest of the staff."

"Poor John! You must be quite famished. Surely the housekeeper might have given you a slice of toast, or a cup of coffee!"

"No, Mrs. Holland feels that having to go hungry until luncheon will teach me to be more prompt in the future." Pickett's efforts to eliminate any trace of bitterness from his voice were not entirely successful.

Lady Fieldhurst's bosom swelled with righteous indignation. "Oh, does she, indeed? I should like to know where she came by the idea that she might order my servants about and discipline them willy-nilly!"

"She has a point, really." Pickett was not quite certain which sounded the most jarring: hearing Lady Fieldhurst refer to him as her servant, or hearing himself come to the housekeeper's defense. "House rules, and all that, you know—"

"House rules be hanged! You must be famished." She dug into her reticule and withdrew a few coins. "Here, take this and buy yourself something to eat at the Pig and Whistle. You will want to keep up your strength if you are to examine the body upon our return. That is why you wished to stop at the church, is it not?"

"It is, my lady, but I have money of my own. I won't take yours."

She would have insisted, but something in his voice and in the set of his jaw made her reconsider. She had not realized until that moment how much of his independence he had been obliged to give up in order to accommodate her request for anonymity. She suspected his pride was still stinging from whatever tongue-lashing the housekeeper had given him, and resolved not to add to his burden any more than she must.

"Very well." She dropped the coins back into her reticule, where they landed with a soft *clink*. "I shall meet you at the Pig and Whistle when I've done with my shopping. I hope you enjoy your belated breakfast; you deserve no less after sacrificing the morning in a futile exercise."

"I wouldn't call it futile, exactly," Pickett said thoughtfully. "I surprised a fellow scavenging among the ruins—or perhaps I should say *he* surprised *me*. I wonder if you may have seen him? Dark, slender, quite young—"

She had to laugh at this description. "If you found him 'quite young,' he must have been little more than a babe in arms!"

"I'm not as young as all that!" protested Pickett.

"I seem to recall your once telling me that you were four-and-twenty."

"And you, I'll wager, are not a day over thirty."

"Thirty!" protested Lady Fieldhurst, offended as only a lady can be whose age has been estimated at greater than her actual years. "I'll have you know I am but six-and-twenty!"

"I stand corrected," said Pickett with a smug smile. "You are a whole two years my senior, in fact."

"Oh, you tricked me! Unfair!" cried her ladyship.

"But effective."

"You are wandering from the subject," Lady Fieldhurst informed him with a haughty sniff that did not fool Pickett for one moment. "You say he was dark. Do you mean dark hair, or dark complexion?"

"Both. Swarthy skin, black hair worn long, shabby clothes, and none too clean."

"And so naturally you thought he must be an acquaintance of mine!"

Pickett's lips twitched, but he resisted the urge to reply in kind. Alone with her, away from the trappings of wealth and rank, it was all too easy to forget the difference between their respective stations and tease her as he might Lucy, the Covent Garden strumpet whose services he gently but firmly declined on a regular basis. He doubted the viscountess would appreciate the comparison. Perhaps he should have taken her money after all, to remind him of his place.

"I didn't mean to suggest you'd asked him to tea," he said. "I thought perhaps you might have seen someone who looked like him—a laborer on the estate, perhaps, or a vagrant along the road."

"No, I can't say that I—wait! Sir Gerald complained of gypsies in the Home Wood, and Mr. Danvers said they had been stealing his chickens, and he had purchased a gun to frighten them away. Could your dark stranger be a gypsy, do you suppose?"

Pickett regarded her with mingled respect and admiration. "I think it not only possible, but very likely. I thank you."

"What do you plan to do now?"

"I don't know. I daresay it will depend on what I find at the church."

They were now climbing the hill rising up from the opposite bank of the river, and eventually the rooftops and chimneys of the village came into view. Pickett, seeing that the time for private conversation was at an end, fell behind once more to the discreet distance expected of a servant.

To her consternation, Lady Fieldhurst felt strangely bereft without the warmth of his arm beneath her fingers. *You had best have a care,* she chided herself, *or you will turn into one of those pathetic creatures so desperate for male companionship that they will fling themselves at anything in breeches!* Yet she could not deny a certain satisfaction in the knowledge that they resided beneath the same roof. *And why not?* came the inevitable mental scold.

You are dwelling among strangers, in a house only a stone's throw from where a gentle parson met a gruesome death. It would be a very odd woman indeed who did not take comfort in the presence of a Bow Street Runner. The very idea that her pleasure in John Pickett's nearness might have more to do with his person than with his profession was too absurd to contemplate.

Chapter 5

A Visit to the Church

"What I shall do with it all, I have no idea," complained Lady Fieldhurst some time later, as they trudged down the road leading away from the village. "One can always use gloves and handkerchiefs, but as for the bonnet, I can't even wear it for another nine months. I have defied convention enough by putting off my blacks far too early; provoke it further by wearing colors before the year is out, I dare not!"

Pickett, who had the honor of transporting said bonnet, along with her ladyship's numerous smaller purchases, picked up his pace to catch up with her. "Then—if you'll pardon my presumption—why did you buy it?"

"So that you might have the privilege of carrying it," she said, albeit not without sympathy for the Bow Street Runner reduced to the rôle of beast of burden. "Having announced that you would accompany me, I had to provide myself with sufficient purchases to justify your presence."

Pickett paused long enough to transfer the strings of the bandbox, which had been banging against his shin for the better part of the journey, to his other hand. "Always happy to be of service."

"Come now, you must confess, this is better than skulking about the church in the middle of the night, is it not?"

Pickett, recalling one memorable occasion when his candle had gone out while he was searching a crypt and the stygian darkness that had enveloped him on that occasion, could not deny it. He glanced at the viscountess to concede the point and found her regarding him speculatively.

"Still, it is a pity to let such a fetching bonnet go to waste," she said. "Is there a female among your acquaintance who might like to have it?"

He considered the various females of his acquaintance. Lucy of Covent Garden fame would be in alt to receive such a gift, but as he was doing his best to discourage her embarrassingly obvious designs upon his person, it would be reckless in the extreme to present her with such a stimulus. Likewise Molly, although heaven knew he could use an ally in the servants' hall. He thought fleetingly of presenting it to Mrs. Holland, but rejected this notion out of hand; aside from the likelihood that she would consider such a gesture a form of bribery, she might well accuse him of theft and see him clapped in the roundhouse.

There was another female, however, about whom he need have no qualms. Mrs. Catchpole, who allowed him to hire the rooms above her shop, and who also cooked and cleaned for him, had much to bear with his comings and goings at all hours of the day or night. It was past time that he gave her some token of his appreciation.

"Yes, I know someone who would be delighted to have it," he said at last.

"Excellent! Then you may give it to her with my compliments," said Lady Fieldhurst although, in truth, she did not understand why this solution, in every way so satisfactory, should put her quite out of temper.

At length they crossed the bridge and began the gentle climb toward the church, Lady Fieldhurst picking her way somewhat gingerly through the muddier spots, as Pickett's arms were too full to allow him to steady her. As they reached the doorstep, he shifted his burden under one arm and tugged open the heavy oak door, which groaned as if protesting the coming desecration. The inside of the church was cool and so dark that it took a moment for Pickett's eyes to adjust sufficiently to pick out the carved angels over the altar.

"They are lovely, are they not?" remarked Lady Fieldhurst, following his gaze upward. "According to Mr. Danvers, all the carving was done by local artisans."

"They give me the creeps," said Pickett, his voice echoing off the stone walls. "Almost as if they know what I'm about to do, and they disapprove."

"You are trying to see that justice is done. Surely they could not disapprove of that."

Lady Fieldhurst, who along with the Hollingshead family had attended a strained and solemn service conducted by Mr. Meriwether on the Sunday following the vicar's death, was sufficiently familiar with the church to locate the vestry, where a plain wooden casket rested on a heavy deal table. A handful of wilting wildflowers lay on top, a pathetic and yet touching tribute to the vicar's popularity with his flock. Pickett piled Lady Fieldhurst's parcels against the wall and took himself off to plunder the sexton's shed. He soon returned bearing an iron crowbar.

"You'd best guard the door," said Pickett, stripping off his coat for greater freedom of movement. "If anyone comes up the path, head him off."

In truth, his concern was less for being caught than for the viscountess to be subjected to a sight too gruesome for a lady's eyes. He had half expected her to protest his rather cavalier dismissal, but she accepted her assigned rôle readily enough and left the vestry with a swiftness suggesting relief.

Alone in the room, Pickett removed the floral offering from the casket and laid it on the floor beside Lady Fieldhurst's parcels, then set to work with the crowbar. Every nail seemed to scream like a soul in torment. Five years earlier, when he'd spent his days hauling coal for his supper, the task would have seemed as nothing, but since joining the Bow Street force, he had become accustomed to using his brains more than his back. By the time he had removed the nails from one length of the coffin, he was breathing heavily, and his shirt clung damply to his skin in spite of the coolness of the room. He paused for a moment to catch his breath before going to work on the other side, when in the silence he heard the groan of the door hinges, followed by Lady's Fieldhurst's cry of determined gaiety, "Why, Mr. Meriwether! Just the person I most wished to see!"

The curate said something—Pickett could not distinguish the words—and Lady Fieldhurst replied, "I should love for you to show me about the churchyard, if you can spare the time. I daresay the Hollingshead vault is well worth a look—"

Her voice faded as the heavy door closed. Her ladyship had surpassed herself at her appointed task, but Pickett had no idea how long she might be able to hold the curate at bay. He returned to his task with renewed urgency, thankful for the thick stone walls that must surely block the sound of the nails' resistance.

At last the final nail surrendered, and Pickett pushed the heavy lid aside. His nostrils were immediately assailed by the stench of smoke, mingled with another, more organic odor whose source he preferred not to dwell upon. It would have been better perhaps had he chosen to forego breakfast that morning, for he feared he might surrender it at any moment. Choking down a paroxysm of dry retches, he staggered to the open door and took great gulps of fresh air from the nave. Above the altar, the carved angels stared serenely down at him as if to remind him that the vicar had no further need of the foul thing in the wooden box, for he now resided in a better place. Steadied somewhat, Pickett turned back to the vestry, pausing only long enough to retrieve a handkerchief from his coat pocket and tie it over his nose and mouth before returning to the open casket.

He could not recall having heard Mr. Danvers described as a bald man, but any hair the vicar had possessed had burned away in the fire, revealing an oddly misshapen head. Pickett forced himself to investigate further, and what he found left no room for doubt.

"I have to hand it to you, my lady," he said, addressing the viscountess as if she were still in the room. "I've never yet known a house fire to bash a man's head in."

Outside in the churchyard, Lady Fieldhurst encouraged Mr. Meriwether to point out the gravesite selected for the vicar's interment, inquiring about every tombstone along the way. It would help, she reflected, if she had some idea of how long she must keep the curate occupied for her *faux* footman to complete his grisly task. The Hollingshead vault should provide fodder enough for several minutes of conversation, and with this end in view, she allowed him to lead her toward the carved stone structure. Before they reached it, however, her attention was caught by a tiny headstone all but hidden beneath mounds of purple and yellow blossoms. The stone itself was not new—the date carved on its face indicated it had been placed there twenty-two years previously—but the painstaking care and the abundance of flowers suggested that someone still mourned the infant buried here two decades earlier.

"How lovely, and how sad," said Lady Fieldhurst, bending down to read the inscription. "Whose is it?"

But even as she asked the question, she saw the answer: Edward, infant son of Sir Gerald and Lady Anne Hollingshead, 9 September 1786.

"Their first child," explained Mr. Meriwether. "He was stillborn only a few months after their marriage."

Lady Fieldhurst thought of her own childlessness and the

sense of loss she had felt every month when her courses had come. "Sad," she said again. "How thankful they must be to have three healthy children to compensate for their loss. But tell me, why is this child not buried in the family vault?"

Mr. Meriwether appeared much struck by this simple query. "Now that you mention it, I have never heard an explanation. I believe there are those who do not believe an infant is truly human until he quickens in the womb. Sir Gerald and Lady Anne married in July of that same year, so she could hardly—that is to say, her condition would not have progressed—"

"Yes, of course," the viscountess said quickly, sparing the young man's blushes. She suppressed a smile at the thought of what Lady Anne might say, had she known she was being discussed in such a manner.

"Be that as it may," the curate continued, "perhaps the family considered burial in the churchyard, but not the vault, a suitable compromise."

Lady Fieldhurst did not dispute this suggestion but privately felt that whoever had decorated the grave so carefully had no doubts they were honoring the memory of a human being. They had by this time reached the vault, and the curate took her arm as they descended the shallow, moss-covered stairs.

"Watch your step," he cautioned. "They may yet be slippery from the rain."

Once inside, she found herself surrounded by large, shadowy shapes indistinguishable in the semidarkness.

"The one on the immediate right is the present baronet's aunt, Henrietta Hollingshead," said Mr. Meriwether, his voice echoing eerily off the walls. "There is a portrait of her in the hall. She was a celebrated beauty in her day, said to rival the Gunning sisters."

"Yes, I remember seeing the portrait," replied the viscountess, casting a sidelong glance in his direction. "I thought she had a look of Miss Hollingshead about her."

"I believe the resemblance is said to be most marked," conceded the curate. "No doubt that is why Lady Anne looks for Miss Hollingshead to imitate her great-aunt's success next spring when she is presented at Court."

"Indeed? I had received the distinct impression that Miss Hollingshead's ambitions lay in quite another direction."

The curate flushed scarlet and muttered something unintelligible. Lady Fieldhurst, seeing that the young man could not be rushed into confidences, hastened to change the subject.

"But why does Henrietta lie here and not with her husband?"

"Her marriage, though brilliant by worldly standards, was not a happy one. Her high-born husband was given to periodic drunken rages, and when she sought comfort in the arms of another, he killed her lover and would no doubt have done the same to her, had she not contrived to escape. She died of consumption several years later, and on her deathbed extracted a promise from her father to bury her in the family vault rather than return her body to her husband."

"A tragic story," murmured Lady Fieldhurst. "We must hope the present Miss Hollingshead meets a happier fate."

"Indeed."

"But am I correct in thinking that you are related to the Hollingsheads as well, Mr. Meriwether?"

"I am, but I fear the connection does my branch of the family no credit," confessed the curate, taking her ladyship's arm to assist her in stepping over a fallen tombstone. "Early in the last century, a village girl caught the eye of the second baronet's son and heir. When she resisted his efforts at seduction, he offered her marriage. She was of simple yeoman stock, and naïve enough to suppose him to be in earnest."

"And was he not?"

"Indeed not! The Hollingshead baronetcy was only in its

second generation; to make such a *mésalliance* at this juncture would damage the family's social position, perhaps irredeemably. But she, in her ignorance, accepted his proposal. He arranged for a fraudulent ceremony to take place in this very church."

"I think I can guess the rest," Lady Fieldhurst said slowly. "By the time she discovered that she had been deceived, the poor girl was with child."

"Precisely. When the scandal broke, the old baronet was furious. The young man was packed off to the Continent, but there was no such escape for Miss Meriwether—for that was her name. You will have guessed by now that she was my great-grandmother."

Lady Fieldhurst, who had not guessed any such thing, strove to conceal her surprise; fortunately, the curate was by this time so engrossed in his tale that he did not notice.

"Having nowhere else to go, she was obliged to endure her shame before the entire village. She eventually gave birth to a son, whom she named William. To give credit where it is due, the old baronet was good to the boy in his way. He provided for the child's education, and would have placed him with a suitable family, had the boy's mother not insisted on keeping him."

"And what of the child's father?" asked the viscountess, enthralled. "Did she never see him again?"

"No, for he was stabbed in a tavern brawl in Venice not long after the boy was born. She, however, lived to a ripe old age, and never left the village. It is said that she grew quite eccentric in her later years, calling her son Sir William and insisting that the townspeople address her as Lady Hollingshead. She is buried there, beneath the elm tree," he added, pointing toward the corner of the churchyard opposite the Hollingshead vault.

Lady Fieldhurst turned to look in the direction he indicated, and spied a gravestone adorned with a statue of an angel cradling a lamb in her arms. "It is a lovely memorial."

"It was placed there by the Hollingshead family," the curate said. "It cannot have been pleasant for them—these old families frequently have a great deal of pride—but they have always been careful to show the Meriwether branch every kindness."

Lady Fieldhurst, who was well acquainted with the pride of an ancient lineage in the form of her deceased husband and his family, suspected that the Hollingsheads' generosity in this case was motivated less by compassion than by relief to be rid at last of an age-old embarrassment. She thought it politic, however, not to voice this suspicion to the curate.

"I can readily believe it," she said instead. "I seem to recall Miss Hollingshead saying that her father had promised you the living here."

Too late, she recalled that, while Emma Hollingshead had indeed suggested such, the viscountess had not been that young lady's intended audience. It was perhaps fortunate, therefore, that Mr. Meriwether was too caught up in his own embarrassment to have a thought for her ladyship's *faux pas.*

"I should not wish to presume—" stammered the curate, flushing a dull red. "—That is, I fear Miss Hollingshead may have refined too much upon—Sir Gerald made no promises, however much he may have implied—"

Lady Fieldhurst interpreted this disjointed speech to mean that, whatever Sir Gerald may have indicated while Mr. Danvers lived, he was prepared to renege on his word now that both his gift and his daughter were seemingly within Mr. Meriwether's reach. She recalled the conversation at breakfast that morning and did not feel optimistic for the young man's chances. It appeared that for the second time within a century, the generosity of the Hollingshead family toward its bastard branch stopped short of marriage.

"Oh, and whose is that vault in the corner?" asked the

viscountess, partly to spare the young man's blushes, and partly to give herself time to digest this new information. "The carving casts the poor baronet's humble memorial quite into the shade!"

Mr. Meriwether chuckled. "I am sure some long-deceased Kendall would be pleased to hear you say so. It is newer by several decades than its neighbor and thus obliged to compensate for its inferior status with superior size and more elaborate ornamentation."

"Kendall?" echoed Lady Fieldhurst. "The same Kendall whom I met at the Hollingsheads' dinner?"

"The very same. It is a friendly rivalry, but a rivalry nonetheless."

"But Lord Kendall not only outranks Sir Gerald, but he holds the position of Justice of the Peace as well. Surely the Kendalls have nothing to prove!"

"One would certainly think not, but so it is with these old County families."

They had by this time completed the circuit of the churchyard and were now heading back toward the church. The viscountess, uncertain as to whether Pickett would have had time to complete his task, cast about in her mind for some excuse for delay.

"And what of the other gentleman at dinner, Mr. Carrington?" she asked. "Has he no ancestor buried here?"

"I fear I know very little about Mr. Carrington," the curate replied. "He settled in the area two years ago, having spent his career abroad—with the East India Company, I believe."

"Has he no wife? No child?"

Mr. Meriwether shook his head. "No, nor ever has had, for anything I have ever heard to the contrary."

This attempt at procrastination proving fruitless, Lady Fieldhurst had no alternative but to follow the curate back to the church. As they rounded the corner, she saw Pickett, looking a bit green about the gills, awaiting her at the door.

"My poor John, I daresay you must have quite given me up. The fault must be Mr. Meriwether's, for he has been showing me about the churchyard and telling me the most fascinating tales about its inhabitants!"

"I beg your pardon, my lady," said the curate, taking this accusation at face value. "I supposed you to be unaccompanied."

"Not at all! I have been to the village, and John was charged with carrying my parcels. I fear my purchases must have been too much for him, for he became quite overcome with the heat, and so has been resting within the church. It is so very pleasant and cool inside, as you no doubt are aware."

Mr. Meriwether made suitable inquiries into Pickett's health (to which he made reassuring, if not very convincing, replies) and bade the viscountess good day. Lady Fieldhurst, setting off up the hill with Pickett at her heels, waited until the curve of the road hid the church from view, then fell into step beside him and slipped her gloved hand through the curve of his arm.

"Are you all right?" she asked, regarding him searchingly. "You look perfectly dreadful!"

"If you think I look bad, you should have seen Mr. Danvers."

"I am very glad I did not!" said the viscountess with feeling. "But I hope you found what you were looking for, for Mr. Meriwether confirmed that the vicar is to be buried tomorrow."

"Excellent work, my lady! I thank you."

Lady Fieldhurst could not have said why this simple tribute should feel so very gratifying, but such was undoubtedly the case. "For what, pray, am I being thanked? For obtaining the information, or holding the curate at bay?"

"Both—and for acting on your suspicions, for they were quite right. Mr. Danvers did not burn to death. In fact, if I were to hazard a guess, I should say he died from a blow to the head."

"A blow to the head?" echoed her ladyship incredulously.

"But what of the gunshot I heard?"

Pickett frowned thoughtfully. "That's what puzzles me. I suppose a ball to the head at close range could crush the skull in such a way, and yet the location of the injury seems wrong. If Mr. Danvers were seated, perhaps, or his assailant were much taller than he—tell me, my lady, do you plan to attend the burial service tomorrow?"

"I? Why, no! Even if I had been well acquainted with Mr. Danvers, it would hardly be appropriate for a woman to be present on such an occasion."

Pickett, who had more than once witnessed members of the gentler sex tearing out one another's hair in an effort to procure the best vantage point from which to view a public hanging, did not attempt to persuade her. "Very well, then, you had best send me as your emissary."

"I was not aware that I needed an emissary."

"Of course you do," he insisted, warming to this idea. "Someone must be present tomorrow to pay last respects to the vicar on your behalf—uphold the honor of the Fieldhursts, and all that. Barring any male relations—"

"Come now, this is doing it much too brown!" she chided, her suspicions by this time fully roused. "You, of all people, know enough about the Fieldhursts to have no illusions as to their honor. You want to attend the funeral for your own purposes, whatever they are."

His smile grew sheepish. "Very well, I admit it."

"What do you expect to find?"

"I don't know—quite possibly nothing. But I would like to see all the suspects—or as many of them as possible—gathered in one place. I'm limited by not being able to question them directly—"

"For which you have me to thank," acknowledged her ladyship ruefully.

"—So I have to draw what conclusions I can from each person's public behavior. It seems to me that a murderer attending his victim's funeral is likely to be very much aware that he is giving a public performance. He may unintentionally give something away."

"Say no more!" beseeched the viscountess, throwing up her hands. "By all means, attend the funeral as my emissary. With any luck, the murderer will be overcome with remorse and confess on the spot, and you may leave my employ before I become quite accustomed to being ordered about by my servants!"

Chapter 6
In Which John Pickett Glimpses the Future

"Forasmuch as it hath pleased Almighty God of his great mercy to take unto himself the soul of our dear brother here departed, we therefore commit his body to the ground; earth to earth, ashes to ashes, dust to dust; in sure and certain hope of the Resurrection . . ."

As the minister's voice rose and fell on the morning breeze, Pickett glanced around at the assembled mourners. Chief among them was Mr. Meriwether, most conspicuous for the fact that he was not conducting the service. That honor, according to Lady Fieldhurst's gleanings in the village, had fallen to the rector of a neighboring parish. And so, with no official duties to perform, the curate now stood at the head of the casket wearing a black armband and a look of tightly controlled anguish. Pickett could not help wondering whether the young man's misery was due to grief at the loss of his mentor, or despair at having committed the sin of murder, only to find himself no closer to the incumbency—or to the daughter of the house—than he was before.

On the other side of the coffin, Sir Gerald Hollingshead stood with his hands clasped behind his back, rocking back and forth on his heels as if impatient to have the unpleasant business behind him. The somber black of his mourning attire made an odd contrast with Sir Gerald's ruddy complexion. Indeed, it seemed almost a pity that ladies were excluded from the burial service; the dignified Lady Anne would have done justice to the solemnity of the occasion far better than her husband the sportsman.

Young Philip Hollingshead stood next to his father, wearing the sullen expression unique to adolescent males. Pickett noted the lad's bloodshot eyes, and suspected they were the result not of remorse, but of over imbibing. Youthful indiscretion, he wondered, or an attempt to drown a guilty conscience? It occurred to Pickett that Emma Hollingshead's various swains were not the only ones with motive for murder. Surely a disgruntled youth might fancy himself well rid of the parson who threatened to put an end to his pleasures. Granted, it was not a strong motive, but Pickett had known men who were killed for less cause, by assailants of even more tender years than Master Philip. He pushed aside the possibility as an unlikely one but not before making a mental note to see what he could discover about the bottles missing from Sir Gerald's stores.

Most of the other mourners were strangers to Pickett, men of the village whom he had never seen at Hollingshead Place. Upon closer inspection, however, he was able to identify a few of them based on Lady Fieldhurst's descriptions. The rather foppish young man glowering at the curate could only be Mr. Kendall, his would-be rival for Miss Hollingshead's affections. Based on this assumption, the older man beside him (more conservatively dressed, yet possessing the same Roman nose and strong chin) must be his father, Lord Kendall, Justice of the Peace. The swarthy gentleman standing to the curate's left was most likely Mr. Carrington, about whose life so little was known.

Some slight movement out of the corner of his eye caught Pickett's attention, and he looked around. There, pressed against the weathered stone wall of the church and almost blending into its shadow, was the same gypsy lad he had surprised in the ruins of the vicarage. Across the width of the churchyard, the dark brown gazes of the two young men locked, one suspicious, the other defiant. Pickett had no doubt the gypsy recognized him in spite of his powdered hair and servant's livery. He gauged the distance between them, calculating whether or not he could cover it with anything approaching discretion. He was about to make his move when the rector began to pray, and Pickett was obliged to make a show of bowing his head.

When he looked up again, the young man was gone.

Lady Fieldhurst stood at the window of her bedchamber, from which vantage point she could just make out the little group of mourners assembled in the churchyard. It was foolish, she knew, to think that she might see anything of interest from this distance, yet that fact had not prevented her from making repeated treks to the window and back ever since the funeral party had first set out from Hollingshead Place. At last, annoyed with both herself and her fruitless occupation, she abandoned the bedchamber and made her way downstairs to the drawing room, a rather cheerless salon whose principal charm lay in the fact that its windows faced west, offering no view of the churchyard. Two members of the household were here before her. Miss Susannah Hollingshead pounded out a mournful piece on the pianoforte, while her governess sat in the corner perusing a thick sheaf of papers through red-rimmed eyes. Miss Grantham looked up as Lady Fieldhurst entered the room and greeted the viscountess with a slightly watery smile.

"Mr. Danvers's history, I presume?" asked Lady Fieldhurst, indicating the stack of papers in the governess's lap.

Miss Grantham gave a mournful sniff. "Poor Mr. Danvers's prose is somewhat ponderous, I fear, but under such tragic circumstances, it seems the least I can do."

"By no means the least, Miss Grantham," the viscountess

said warmly. "I can think of no greater tribute you might offer him."

And no greater sacrifice, she added mentally, if the vicar's writing was even half as pedantic as his conversation.

"It is very kind of you to say so, my lady. I confess, it would give me great satisfaction to think of Mr. Danvers's life's work being published posthumously. I feel it behooves me to prepare the manuscript for publication, should his heirs choose to pursue such a course." She gave a sigh. "I fear it is all they may expect to inherit from him, as everything else was destroyed in the fire."

"Who is his heir, pray?" asked the viscountess.

Miss Grantham shook her head. "Some niece or nephew, I daresay, or perhaps a distant cousin. Mr. Danvers never married, so there is no direct descendant."

The conversation was interrupted by the arrival of Lady Anne, clad in a sober but obviously expensive morning gown of plum-colored silk. "My dear Lady Fieldhurst, I wonder if I might beg a word with you? It concerns your footman."

Miss Grantham, correctly interpreting this question as a dismissal of herself and her charge, arranged her papers into a neat stack and rose to her feet. Miss Susannah banged out one last dolorous chord, then followed her preceptress from the room with uncharacteristic docility.

Lady Fieldhurst, in the meantime, watched their exit with growing apprehension. Had Mr. Pickett said or done something to betray himself? Worse, had Lady Anne observed their arm-in-arm jaunt to the village and drawn her own conclusions?

"Yes?" the viscountess prompted, as the door closed behind the governess and her pupil. "What did you wish to say?"

"As you know, my daughter Emma will be presented at Court next spring and will have her Season in London."

"I'm sure she will be a great success," said Lady Fieldhurst, not quite certain what this had to do with John Pickett.

"Thank you. Her father and I have high hopes for her. But as you know, it is crucial to present the right image. Besides her wardrobe to refurbish, there is the matter of opening up the town house and hiring more fashionable servants than can be found in the country. As your mourning obliges you to live very quietly at present, I wonder if you would object to my speaking to your John about coming to us?"

Revelation dawned, but it brought no relief. In fact, the prospect of Mr. Pickett remaining in Yorkshire at the beck and call of the Hollingshead ladies, pursuing his investigations alone while she herself returned to London, was in its own way quite as disturbing as discovering that he had been exposed as an imposter.

Seeing that her hostess awaited an answer, Lady Fieldhurst swallowed hard and found her tongue with some difficulty. "Am—Am I to understand, Lady Anne, that you wish to *hire* John?"

"Only if you have no objections, my dear. As you know, it can add a great deal to a lady's consequence to have a tall and handsome young footman accompanying her carriage."

"I don't find him overly handsome," muttered Lady Fieldhurst pettishly.

"His nose has obviously been broken at some point, but although that must have been a most unpleasant experience for the poor fellow, I cannot see that it affects his desirability as a footman," continued Lady Anne, undaunted. "In fact, it often happens that such flaws add to the appeal of a masculine countenance."

As the viscountess could find nothing to say to refute this observation, Lady Anne took her silence as permission granted.

"Very well, then, if you have no objection, I shall speak to him at the earliest opportunity. Thank you, my dear. I assure you, your generosity will not be soon forgotten."

If Lady Fieldhurst was impatient for Pickett's return before, she was now frantic. He should at least be warned of Lady Anne's intentions before that redoubtable lady accosted him, so that he might be better prepared to gratefully but firmly turn down her generous offer.

The only trouble was that Lady Fieldhurst was not at all certain that he would turn it down. In fact, he might welcome the opportunity to stay in Yorkshire for as long as he liked, insinuating himself into the servants' confidence as a member of the household, and learning all the family's secrets. She might return to London at her leisure and need have no further contact with him at all. Well! If that was his notion of gratitude, when he would not have even known about the case at all had she not sent for him, then Lady Anne might have him with her blessing!

It was in this volatile frame of mind that Lady Fieldhurst entered the dining room, where most of the mourners had convened for a sober meal. Pickett stood behind the viscountess's chair, and the Hollingsheads' own footmen were stationed at intervals around the table. The accoutrements were perhaps more suited to dinner than to the noon meal, but the visiting rector must needs be fed before setting out for his own parish, and Sir Gerald, within whose gift the living lay, was the logical person to extend this hospitality. Glancing around the table at the solemn group, the viscountess noted that the party was very nearly the same as the one assembled for dinner on that fateful night. Besides the cleric, the only addition was the doctor—the same man who, in his official capacity of coroner, had erroneously identified the cause of death. On the debit side, the schoolroom party was absent, as were Lady Kendall and Miss Hollingshead.

"I must commend you for your words of comfort, Mr. Greenfield," the curate addressed the visiting cleric. Lady Fieldhurst could not but admire the young man's poise, for only a slight stiffening of his spine betrayed how much effort it cost him to remain gracious in the face of such a snub.

"Yes, yes, a good end to a bad business," blustered Sir Gerald.

"Thank you, Sir Gerald, Mr. Meriwether," replied the rector. "It is always difficult to know what to say in the face of such a tragedy. I trust that all who knew him must find comfort in the knowledge that Mr. Danvers has gone on to a better place."

"Then it is no wonder Mr. Meriwether found his words so encouraging," put in Robert Kendall, casting a sly glance in the curate's direction, "for he hopes to follow his mentor's example and go on to a better place himself. Though not the same one, it goes without saying."

Philip Hollingshead uttered a short bark of laughter which he turned, not very convincingly, into a cough.

Mr. Meriwether's jaw tightened, but he remained staunchly silent. Sir Gerald harrumphed into his napkin, while Lord Kendall glared at his son and heir, his brow lowering ominously. The doctor, attempting to pour oil on troubled waters, rushed into speech, but his choice of subject betrayed his recognition of the bone of contention between the two young men.

"As always, Lady Anne, you set an excellent table, but I confess its magnificence is dimmed by the absence of your charming daughter. Where, pray, is Miss Hollingshead?"

"Emma is confined to her room with a sick headache," Lady Anne said placidly, seemingly unaware of the tension about the table. "I wonder if you might consent to look in on her before you go?"

"Certainly, certainly," the doctor assured her. "I daresay her nerves are overset by the sad activities of the day. A dose of laudanum should help her rest, and she should feel much more the thing when she awakens."

As the doctor made his diagnosis, Pickett leaned forward to refill Lady Fieldhurst's glass. She attempted to catch his eye and convey a whispered warning, but was preempted by Lord Kendall, who addressed her with a query.

"How much longer are we to enjoy your company, Lady Fieldhurst? I regret that you have not seen us at our best. I fear you must be eager to abandon us for London."

"I can hardly fault you for the weather, Lord Kendall, nor for Mr. Danvers's tragic demise," she assured him.

"My dear Lady Fieldhurst, I hope we can persuade you to stay long enough to explore some of the sights of Yorkshire," put in Lady Anne. "Mother Shipton's Cave, for instance, or John of Gaunt's castle."

"An excellent notion!" seconded the rector, his round face beaming with approval. "In times of tragedy, we must not forget the simple pleasures of life, for we are reminded that they can be snatched from us all too quickly."

Lady Fieldhurst readily agreed to this program for her entertainment, for the more she could prolong her visit, the less incentive John Pickett would have for entering Lady Anne's employ as a means of extending his investigations.

It was not until the first course was ending that Lady Fieldhurst saw her opportunity to warn him of her hostess's intentions. As Pickett removed her plate, the viscountess quite deliberately dropped her napkin on the floor at his feet. He bent to retrieve it, an action which brought his ear in close proximity to her mouth.

"You'd best have a care," she murmured. "Lady Anne intends to make you an offer of employment."

"Very good, my lady," replied Pickett, at his most wooden.

As an answer, it was a great deal too ambiguous for Lady

Fieldhurst's liking. Did he mean "very good" as in "thank you for warning me in advance," or "very good" as in "what an excellent notion"?

"Well?" she demanded *sotto voce* as he shook the napkin open with a flourish and replaced it in her lap. "What do you intend to do?"

"I think," he said with a twinkle in his eye that belied his expressionless tone, "that I shall have my fortune told."

A servant's life, Pickett reflected, was not an easy one. He found himself singularly ill-suited to it, for he was too much in the habit of being his own man to easily adapt to arranging his life for the convenience of even so charming a mistress as Lady Fieldhurst. While he was ultimately answerable to his magistrate, Mr. Colquhoun, for his actions, he was not at that gentleman's beck and call twenty-four hours a day. In the end, it was not until dinner was finished and the last teaspoon washed, dried, and stored away with the family silver that he was at last able to make good his escape. He set off in the direction of the river, doing his best to look as if he had been dispatched to the village on an errand for the viscountess. Once he rounded the bend which hid Hollingshead Place from sight, however, he veered sharply off the river road and headed for the woods.

The stands of ancient oaks grew thick, their green canopies meeting overhead to block out most of the remaining sunlight. Pickett, straining to see his way in the semidarkness, had ventured only a few yards when he almost ran over a fellow sojourner.

"Oh, how you startled me!" cried a childishly high-pitched voice. "You are Lady Fieldhurst's footman, are you not?"

Pickett, his eyes growing more accustomed to the dark, recognized the younger daughter of the house, a schoolroom miss of about fourteen. "John Pickett, at your service," he said, bowing deeply from the waist. "And you, I think, are Miss Hollingshead."

"Yes—well, actually, my sister Emma is Miss Hollingshead," she admitted grudgingly. "I am Miss Susannah. But I will be Miss Hollingshead after she marries, which must be soon, now that Cousin Colin will become vicar."

It would be disgraceful, he knew, for him to pump this innocent child, but his opportunities for first-hand information were few, thanks to his present charade. He could not afford to pass up such a chance. "Forgive me, Miss Susannah, but I was under the impression that your sister was going to make a brilliant match in London."

"Mama wishes her to, because Mama was the daughter of an earl, and so she wants Emma to marry an earl, too. But I heard Emma tell Mama that she would marry Cousin Colin or no one, and although Miss Grantham thinks that Emma is gentle and soft-spoken just as a lady should be, I know she can be amazingly stubborn when she chooses. And I have known her a great deal longer than Miss Grantham has!"

"I see. And what does your papa say?"

"He only says he will not be rushed into naming the new vicar. I think he does not want to see Emma made unhappy, but then, he does not want Mama to be unhappy, either, and one or the other of them *must* be. Poor Papa!" Her expression grew pensive. "Poor Papa."

Pickett said solemnly that he did not envy Sir Gerald such a difficult decision.

"Nor do I!" Miss Susannah concurred vehemently. "At least he will not have such a decision to make where I am concerned."

"No?" Pickett inquired with careful nonchalance.

"No, for I am going to the gypsy camp to have my fortune told, and I daresay the cards will tell me whom I am to marry. Perhaps I should ask about Emma, too, while I am about it."

"By happy coincidence, I am on my way to the same place. Will you accept my escort, Miss Susannah? I cannot think Miss Grantham would like your wandering about the woods alone."

This observation provoked a look of such guilt that Pickett surmised the governess was blissfully unaware of her charge's present whereabouts.

"She would not like it at all—if she knew where I was," admitted Susannah, confirming Pickett's worst suspicions.

"In fact, you gave Miss Grantham the slip," he observed.

"You won't tell, will you?" pleaded the girl. "She confined me to my room for gossiping with the servants, except that I was doing no such thing, only Jem—the stable boy, you know—was telling me the most *thrilling* story about putting out the fire at the vicarage, but Miss Grantham ordered me to my room and told me no man would ever wish to marry me if I did not learn to behave like a lady. But Miss Grantham *always* behaves like a lady, and no man has ever wished to marry her, either, so if it really makes no difference in the end, I don't see why I shouldn't at least have *fun!* And so, since I am already in disgrace for gossiping with Jem (even though it was really no such thing), I might as well run away and have my fortune told, for I have been wanting to do so *forever,* and no one will let me, and I might just as well be punished for two things as one, do you not think so?"

Pickett, following this impassioned speech with some difficulty, thought it behooved him to make what inquiries he could at the gypsy camp, and return Miss Susannah Hollingshead to the care of her governess with all possible speed. Gradually the woods thinned until they stopped at the edge of a clearing where some half dozen dirty canvas tents had been set up. A fire burned in front of one of these, heating the pungent contents of a black cast-iron cauldron. At the front flap of another, a woman plucked a chicken (stolen from the vicarage, no doubt) with brisk, efficient movements. Three men huddled beyond the campsite, smoking crude pipes and staring at the intruders with thinly veiled hostility. As Pickett and his charge watched, a stooped crone emerged from one of the tents, plopped down on a three-legged stool, and stirred the pot with a large wooden spoon, mumbling beneath her breath as she performed her task. Watching her, Pickett was forcibly reminded of the witches' scene from a recent Covent Garden production of *Macbeth.*

"Somehow it doesn't look nearly as romantic as I had expected," murmured Miss Susannah, edging closer to him. "In the evenings, when I could open my window and hear the violins and the tambourine, it always sounded so jolly. I thought—I thought—"

"I imagine a young gypsy girl would think *your* life romantic," Pickett pointed out gently. "After all, you live in a grand house, you wear fine clothes—"

"Well?" called out the crone, brandishing her spoon in their direction. "What do ye want?"

Pickett glanced down at Susannah Hollingshead and found her gazing up at him with a look of mute appeal. Clearly, he was designated as spokesperson. He couldn't help wondering how Miss Susannah would have coped with this task had she not happened upon him along the way.

"We would like to have our fortunes told," he informed the crone.

"You'll never get 'em done standing over there."

The crone rose stiffly to her feet and shuffled back into the tent. She remained inside for so long that Pickett began to think she was gone for good. He was just about to suggest to Miss Susannah that they cut their losses and return to the house before her absence was noted, when the old gypsy woman returned, shuffling a stack of cards in her gnarled hands. She sank back down onto the stool with an odd sort of dignity and looked at them expectantly. Pickett, correctly interpreting this as an invitation, took Miss Susannah's arm and approached the old woman.

"Well, my pretty, let's see what the cards have to say," cackled the crone, looking the girl up and down appraisingly.

Pickett glanced down at his companion, and noted with some amusement that Miss Susannah was exceedingly reluctant to claim the long-coveted prize, now that it was within reach. "I'll go first, shall I?" he suggested.

Miss Susannah nodded mutely, and he dropped a silver shilling into the old woman's upturned palm. As the two watched, she laid out the cards in a simple geometric pattern. One by one, she turned them over to reveal, not the familiar clubs, spades, diamonds, and hearts, but strange pictures of cups, coins, swords, and oddly dressed people. She muttered as she studied the peculiar collection, sometimes talking to herself, sometimes to Pickett.

"A man of many secrets . . . the Page of Swords . . . you are on a quest. Much depends upon your success. Hmm . . . the Five of Swords . . . many things, many people will try to lead you astray. You must not let them." The old gypsy fell silent for a long moment, then continued, "There is something else, something you want very badly, but that seems to be out of your reach. The Four of Cups, the Ten of Wands . . . you may yet achieve your heart's desire, but not without great difficulty. The Two and the Four of Pentacles . . . Yes, money is part of the problem, but there are other, even greater obstacles. The Emperor . . . a rich and powerful man who casts a long shadow. The High Priest, another man, one whose good opinion you value. No, not a father. An employer, perhaps . . ."

"His employer is a lady," said Susannah, finding her tongue at last. "The Viscountess Fieldhurst."

"I see," said the old crone, studying Pickett intently. Pickett, who a scant fifteen minutes earlier would have sworn the whole thing was so much balderdash, was seized with the uncomfortable notion that the old gypsy saw far too much. He gave her back look for look, willing himself not to blush, and felt no small sense of relief when she fixed her too-knowing gaze on the girl beside him. As a further sign that she had finished with him, she swept up the cards in a single, surprisingly dexterous, movement and began to lay them out again.

"Six of Swords, Four of Cups . . . Your life is about to change. You must make a journey . . ."

The cryptic tone of Miss Susannah's fortune, if not the particulars, sounded so similar to his own that Pickett decided the gypsy's uncanny accuracy was nothing more than a memorized spiel deliberately vague enough that anyone might find some grain of truth within it. Miss Susannah would, after all, be emancipated from the schoolroom within two or three years; it required no gift of second sight to know that her life would indeed change, or that she would make the obligatory trek to London in search of an eligible husband. Glancing down at the wide-eyed girl eagerly absorbing every word, Pickett had no doubt that intrepid damsel could think of some potential changes or journeys of her own which would lend verisimilitude to the old hag's predictions.

Some slight sound caught his attention, and Pickett looked up to find the same gypsy youth he had seen twice before, first in the burned-out vicarage and more recently at the graveside service that morning, lurking between two tents and watching him warily. As inconspicuously as possible, Pickett detached himself from Susannah's side and edged away. The youth, seeing what he was about, disappeared around the corner of the nearest tent. Pickett quickly reversed direction and circled the tent from the opposite direction, so that the two young men all but collided behind it.

"Wait!" cried Pickett, seizing the youth by the collar when he made as if to run away. "I want a word with you."

"I've got nothing to say to the likes of you," came the sullen reply.

"You were at the burial service this morning. I saw you there."

"So, and what if I was?" spat the youth. "Can't a fellow attend the burial of his own father?"

CHAPTER 7

In Which John Pickett Tries His Hand at Burglary, with Unexpected Results

"Father?" Pickett echoed incredulously. "Cyril Danvers was your *father?*"

The young man's lips twisted in a singularly unpleasant smile. "What else could it mean, when a man sets out alone for India and comes back four years later with an infant boy in tow?"

Strangely, horribly, it made sense. The youth's golden brown skin and thick black hair could easily be the result of a union between an Englishman and a native woman.

Pickett's eyes narrowed. "What is your name?"

"It's obvious, isn't it? I don't have one."

"The gypsies must call you something."

"Will," the youth admitted grudgingly. "I'm called Will Huggins, after my foster father."

"How do you know this? About Mr. Danvers bringing you to England from India, I mean."

"You're a regular Nosey Parker, aren't you? If you must know, my mum told me, right before she died." A shadow crossed his face, and for a moment he looked more like a confused boy than an angry young man. "I know she wasn't really my mum, but I don't know what else to call her."

"When was this?"

He shrugged. "Two, maybe three years ago. Dates don't matter much to the gypsies. I always knew the Hugginses weren't my real folks, Mum nor Dad, neither. They were both fair and short and plump, and I'm—well, look at me. I think my mum knew I'd always wondered, and that's why she decided to tell me, before it was too late."

"What, exactly, did she say?"

Again that shrug, half careless, half defiant. "What I just told you. That Danvers had come back to England after four years in India, bringing a babe almost two years old. That he left me with them, seeing as how they'd lost their own child to the croup, and sent them money twice a year to care for me."

"You say Mrs. Huggins is dead now. What of your foster father?"

"Aye, he went first of all."

"And so you joined the gypsies."

"Why not? There was nothing for me in Little Neddleby anymore. It cost me everything they had left just to bury them proper."

"So you joined the gypsy camp in order to reach your real father."

"Maybe. But I never spoke to him, nor approached him in any way," he added hastily. "So if you're thinking I killed him, you're wrong. I had a couple or three chickens off him, but nothing more."

"I saw you in the ruins of the vicarage," Pickett reminded him.

"Well, and what if I was? If anything survived the fire, wasn't it rightfully mine? Not that I need have bothered," he said bitterly. "There was nothing left but a few pots and pans."

"And a poker," said Pickett. Seeing the youth's sullen expression give way temporarily to puzzlement, he explained, "I tripped over it, trying to catch you."

"You wouldn't have done it, anyway," the lad said with simple pride. "I'm that quick on my feet."

Pickett, who had chased down his share of London's criminal element on foot, smiled but said nothing. A moment later, Miss

Susannah Hollingshead joined him, full of rosy prophecies for her future.

"She says I shall marry a rich man and live in a fine house," Miss Susannah informed Pickett as they retraced their steps through the woods. "But I think she may tell everyone that, for she said the same thing about Emma, and *she* says she will marry Cousin Colin or no one."

Pickett, for his part, found it difficult to work up much enthusiasm for the futures of either of the Hollingshead sisters; he was too distracted by thoughts of the gypsy youth's extraordinary tale. Here, certainly, was a more compelling motive for murder than the curate's star-crossed love for Miss Hollingshead. Suppose Will had, in fact, confronted Mr. Danvers, and had been rebuffed? An idealistic young man, imagining a loving reconciliation and a permanent home, might well react violently to so bitter a disappointment.

Nor could Will's youth excuse him: Pickett had known younger lads to kill and to hang for it. He would not soon forget the sight of a fourteen-year-old going to the gallows sobbing for his mother. While Will was well past the age of fourteen, something about the lonely youth reminded Pickett of the boy he had once been. He found himself hoping someone, *anyone,* else would prove to be the guilty party. He could hear Mr. Colquhoun's most magisterial voice in his head, cautioning him against becoming too personally attached to the subjects of his investigations, and ruefully acknowledged that he was treading dangerously near that fine line. He took some small comfort in the knowledge that, on at least one occasion ten years earlier, Mr. Colquhoun had failed to follow his own advice.

Some time later, Pickett confided his discovery to Lady Fieldhurst in the privacy of her ladyship's bedchamber.

"It seems the good reverend Mr. Danvers was a man with a

secret." He paused, grimacing at the sound of his own words. "I'd best have a care about the company I keep. I'm beginning to sound just like Madame Rosa!"

"Who, pray, is Madame Rosa?" asked the viscountess, all at sea.

"A gypsy fortune-teller."

Lady Fieldhurst gave a delighted crow of laughter. "Did you truly have your fortune told, then? I was certain you must be roasting me!"

"I did, but only as an excuse to go nosing about the gypsy camp."

"And what did Madame Rosa tell you?" the viscountess urged.

Pickett, receiving the full force of her ladyship's sparkling blue eyes and eager smile, had no difficulty in recalling the crone's words. *There is something you want very badly, something just out of your reach . . .*

"That's neither here nor there," said Pickett hastily. "What's more to the purpose is that there is a young hothead in the camp who claims to be Danvers's bast—er, illegitimate child."

"Is there indeed? How very ironic!"

"Ironic? In what way?"

"On the night he died, Mr. Danvers complained at dinner of gypsies stealing his chickens. He had even provided himself with a weapon to frighten them off—the gypsies, I mean, not the chickens."

"I think I saw it," said Pickett, recalling the charred remains of the fowling piece over the mantel. "What's left of it, anyway."

"I merely thought it ironic that, having assured Lady Kendall that night that he had no intention of harming the gypsies, he appears to have been harmed by one of them instead."

"Maybe," Pickett said slowly, "and yet I don't think so."

"Why not? You cannot deny the young man—we are speaking

of a man, are we not? I cannot quite picture a female in the rôle of gypsy hothead."

Pickett smiled. "We are, indeed. Only I would hesitate to call him a man. I daresay Will is still in his teens."

"And you so ancient as you are!" she retorted, returning his smile. "No, no, I am only funning, so pray do not rip up at me about your four-and-twenty years! Tell me instead why young Will could not have killed his natural father."

"I never said he *could* not have done so, only that I don't think he did. As for my reasons—" he hesitated, searching for words. "Call it intuition, if you will, but it seems to me the fellow's asking to get caught. He can't quite bring himself to knock on the front door bold as brass and introduce himself, so he pinches a chicken or two in the hopes of forcing a confrontation the only way he knows how."

"I see," Lady Fieldhurst said slowly. "Mr. Danvers catches the thief and threatens to haul him before the magistrate, and young Will reveals his true identity. At which point the vicar clasps the prodigal to his bosom, and father and son are reunited, nevermore henceforth to be parted. Yes, it is just the sort of romantic story one is inclined to fancy when one is young. But what if Will had, in fact, contrived just such a scenario, only to be rebuffed? Might he not have struck the vicar in anger?"

"He is certainly the sort to react foolishly, possibly even violently," admitted Pickett. "But I think he would stop short of murder."

"What makes you say so?"

"Because," said Pickett, gazing pensively into the fire, "if he kills Mr. Danvers, he kills his last hope. So long as his father is alive, there is some chance, however slight, for a reconciliation."

Lady Fieldhurst found herself wondering what had happened between John Pickett and his father to put that faraway expression in his eyes. "Very well," she said softly, "I concede Will's innocence."

Pickett was immediately recalled to the present. "I never said he was innocent," he reminded her with a wry grin. "He's a chicken thief, by his own admission."

"So, if Will didn't kill Mr. Danvers, who did?"

"I wish I knew. I can't help thinking Will's paternity is mixed up in it somehow, though. If Will found out about it, who's to say someone else hasn't?"

"Do you think Mr. Danvers was being blackmailed, then?"

"Something like that. But in that case, it would have been more likely for the blackmailer to be murdered by the victim, rather than the other way 'round."

Her ladyship frowned thoughtfully. "It would seem so. And yet, whatever his youthful indiscretions, Mr. Danvers seemed to be a good man. What if he had determined to make a public confession of his past sins? Not only would the blackmailer's source of income be eliminated, but his own reputation would be ruined, should the vicar make public that particular aspect of the story."

"An interesting theory, my lady," observed Pickett. "Unfortunately, we'll need solid evidence to make it stick, and most of that appears to have burned up in the vicarage fire."

"What of the blackmailer?" asked her ladyship, pondering a new possibility. "Would he not keep records of payments received?"

"Very likely, if we knew where to look." He noticed her arrested expression. "You've thought of something."

"I think perhaps I have," she said with great deliberation. "At dinner that night, Mr. Danvers asked Sir Gerald if he might speak to him on a matter of some importance. Sir Gerald agreed to see him but, as I recall, changed the subject rather abruptly."

"So you think Sir Gerald may have been the blackmailer, and

the vicar intended to tell him the game was up?"

She shrugged. "It makes as much sense as anything else we've come up with."

Pickett was silent for a long moment, then asked, "Tell me, does Sir Gerald employ a steward?"

"No, he is very much the country gentleman and takes great pride in managing the estate himself. Why? Does it matter?"

"It means he could record income from blackmail payments without having to worry about awkward questions from his steward," he explained. "Whether he actually did so or not remains to be seen. Do you know where Sir Gerald does his bookkeeping?"

"He doesn't have a study, as far as I know, but there is a locked desk in the library. I daresay that would be the most likely place to keep important papers."

"What time does the household usually settle down for the night?"

"Around midnight usually." Her eyes narrowed in suspicion. "John Pickett! Tell me you don't intend to burgle the library!"

He met her accusing look with one of utmost innocence. "I'm not going to *steal* anything."

"You will be careful, won't you?"

"I'll try," he said, crossing the room to the service door. "If I'm not serving at breakfast tomorrow, you'll know I was discovered and thrown into the nearest roundhouse."

He pushed open the panel. As he stepped through the opening, Lady Fieldhurst called, "Oh, John?"

"Yes, my lady?"

Her blue eyes gleamed with mischief. "You never did tell me what Madame Rosa said."

"No, I didn't, did I?" he retorted, and disappeared down the narrow stair.

★ ★ ★ ★ ★

On evenings when there were no dinner guests, the Hollingsheads kept country hours. Dinner was served promptly at five o'clock, and by eight, the household staff had not only finished its own meal, but had washed, dried, and stored away the dishes, down to the last teaspoon. Pickett, having completed his daily duties, was left to while away the remaining hours until midnight as best he might. He retired to his tiny bedchamber in the attic, withdrew his notebook from its hiding place beneath the mattress, and began to make notes.

Having at last committed the curious story of Will's parentage to paper, he flipped back over the previous pages. They were depressingly few. He wished he had not been quite so hasty in agreeing to Lady Fieldhurst's request that he keep his identity secret; it was woefully difficult to gather information when he could not question any member of the household directly. Common sense demanded that he end the charade and inform Lady Fieldhurst that he could not possibly investigate a murder under such a constraint. Unfortunately, his common sense seemed to be in remarkably short supply where her ladyship was concerned.

Gradually, a faint scratching at the door penetrated his consciousness. He snapped the notebook closed and reached for the edge of the mattress, but he was too late. Before he could secret it away out of sight, the door swung open on creaky hinges, and Miss Susannah Hollingshead swept into the room clad in nothing but her white linen nightrail.

"M-Miss Susannah," said Pickett, striving to appear unconcerned, "to what do I owe the honor of this visit?"

"Miss Grantham is being tiresome, so I thought I would come and talk to you."

"Miss Grantham no doubt expects you to be in your bed," Pickett pointed out, casting a wary glance at the half-open door.

If Mrs. Holland should happen to hear feminine accents issuing from the footmen's quarters and come upstairs expecting to catch him and the predatory Molly *in flagrante delicto,* and instead discover him alone with the younger daughter of the house . . . He shuddered, his brain recoiling from a scenario too horrendous to contemplate. "It is quite late, you know."

"Pish tosh!" declared Miss Susannah inelegantly. "It is only eleven o'clock. Emma is allowed to stay up much later, and when she goes to London she will stay out every night dancing until dawn!" She punctuated this statement with a series of whirling steps, arms outstretched.

"Very possibly, but Miss Hollingshead is rather older than you. Your day will come, but in the meantime—"

"Hullo, what's this?" asked Miss Susannah, reaching for the notebook lying on the bed.

"Nothing!" said Pickett, snatching it from her probing fingers. "That is, it's a sort of diary."

She eyed the notebook in his hands speculatively. "Do you write your deepest, most secret thoughts in it?"

He smiled. "Something like that." It was not quite a lie, at any rate.

"Perhaps I should do the same," said Miss Susannah, much struck. "I could write down Madame Rosa's predictions, and then years from now, when I am a married lady, I can read them and see if they came true."

"An excellent notion," seconded Pickett, taking her elbow and steering her toward the door. "You should do so at once, before you forget anything."

She regarded him suspiciously. "Are you trying to get rid of me?"

"Yes, Miss Susannah, I am," he declared with no roundaboutation.

"Why? Don't you like me?"

"What I like is entirely beside the point. If you were discovered here, particularly at this hour and dressed in such a way, you would be locked in your room and given nothing to eat but bread and water, and I would be thrown out of the house on my, er, ear."

"But—" Miss Susannah's protest died on her lips, and her eyes widened. "Do you mean people would think you had *compromised* me?"

Pickett blushed at her frankness but answered with equal candor. "That is exactly what they would think. And, given the circumstances, who could blame them?"

"Well!" declared Miss Susannah, fairly beaming with pride. "That is the nicest thing anyone has ever said to me. Now I feel quite grown up!"

To Pickett's somewhat bewildered relief, she bade him goodnight and left the room without further protest. He waited a few moments to satisfy himself that she was truly gone, then tucked the notebook back into its hiding place and pondered how best to spend the hours remaining until the household had settled down for the night. If he had harbored fears regarding the coming foray into housebreaking, these had now been laid to rest: surely the night could hold no terrors greater than his recent *tête-à-tête* with Miss Susannah Hollingshead.

He scratched his itching scalp, and dusted the resulting snowfall from the shoulders of his livery. He wished he might brush the white powder from his hair but was obliged to abandon this tempting thought; the last thing he needed at the moment was a fit of sneezing to awaken his fellow servants.

In the end, he paced the floor and watched the clock until at last, an hour past midnight, he picked up his candle and cautiously opened the creaking door. Shielding the feeble flame with his hand, he slowly picked his way down the stairs. He had reached the second floor, where the family's bedchambers were located, when he saw the faint glow of another candle. Someone was climbing the stairs from the floor below.

Pickett blew out his candle and ducked quickly into the nearest doorway, from which vantage point he could watch from the shadows as the nocturnal wanderer moved through the house in a manner which could only be described as suspicious. Not until the stealthy figure had drawn abreast of his hiding place could Pickett identify the slender form of Philip Hollingshead. In his right hand, the boy carried a brass candlestick holding a single taper; in his left, he clutched the neck of a bottle whose contents glowed in the candlelight like topaz. Apparently young Philip had tired of wine, and was now making inroads into his father's cognac. The breast of his coat bulged with what was apparently yet another bottle of contraband spirits. In his eagerness to escape to his bedroom with this prize, he did not so much as glance in Pickett's direction.

Pickett waited until his candle disappeared around the landing above, then let out a long breath. If nothing else, he had solved the mystery of the bottles missing from the wine cellar. Unfortunately, he could not report this newfound knowledge to his superiors belowstairs without being castigated as a talebearer.

Having extinguished his own candle, he was obliged to complete his descent in the dark, which slowed him down considerably. He had almost reached the library door when a female voice hissed, "At last! I had begun to think you had fallen asleep."

"My lady!" Pickett's answering whisper seemed scarcely louder than the pounding of his heart. "What are you doing here?"

"Surely you didn't expect that I would allow you to commit burglary alone?"

"That is *exactly* what I expected—and what you should have done." But in spite of his protests, Pickett found himself steering her into the library and shutting the door behind them.

"I would not have closed my eyes all night for worrying about you." Being more familiar with the layout of the room than he, she groped about in the dark room for a flint, then fumbled with the candle until it flared to life. "But what kept you so long? I have been waiting this half hour and more."

"The corridors were a bit more crowded than I had anticipated." Seeing her ladyship's puzzled expression, Pickett explained about his late-night visit from the younger daughter of the house and about the clandestine activities of its son and heir.

To his surprise, the viscountess found the former the more intriguing of the two. "Why, John!" she exclaimed. "I believe you have made a conquest!"

He frowned. "What are you talking about?"

"Pray do not be so modest! It is obvious to the meanest intelligence that Miss Susannah Hollingshead is in the throes of a schoolgirl *tendre.*"

"Nonsense! All I did was walk with her as far as the gypsy camp and back."

"Yes, you took her to see Madame Rosa when no one else would, and you didn't report her indiscretion to her governess. Furthermore, you were too gallant to compromise her when given the opportunity—"

Pickett's blushes outshone the candle in his hand. "What rubbish!"

"And now you are doubtless her *beau ideal.* I am sorry if you don't like it, John, but I fear you brought it on yourself."

Pickett closed his eyes, his expression pained. "Just show me the desk, my lady."

"Very well, I shan't tease you anymore, but I hope you will deal gently with her. Schoolgirl *tendres,* however short-lived, can be very keenly felt."

He stammered something so incoherent that she took pity on him and led the way to a mahogany desk positioned before the window to catch the morning sun. At the moment, the long velvet curtains were tightly closed against the darkness, and Pickett gave them an extra tug to make sure the faint illumination from their candles could not be seen from outside. Satisfied, he set his candle on the desk and pulled gently on the top drawer. It was locked, just as Lady Fieldhurst had said.

"Have you a hairpin I can borrow?" he whispered, dropping down onto one knee.

She said nothing but dug her fingers into her hair and withdrew a long pin from the elegantly coiffed curls. He took it from her and inserted it into the lock. Pressing his ear close, he manipulated the hairpin in the lock until he heard a faint click, then withdrew the pin and slid the drawer open.

"A useful talent," murmured the viscountess, observing the proceedings over his shoulder. "Where, pray, did you develop it?"

He grinned sheepishly. "Best not say, perhaps."

At first glance, the drawer appeared to contain nothing but an assortment of old letters. Pickett leafed through these until he uncovered a calf-bound ledger. Before he could remove it from the drawer, a footstep sounded in the hall beyond, and a moment later the doorknob rattled. For one agonizing second, the Runner and the viscountess stared at each other in mutual horror.

The knob turned and the door began to swing open. Lady Fieldhurst was the first to react. Seizing Pickett by the lapels of his borrowed livery, she dragged his head down and covered his mouth with hers.

Chapter 8

In Which Are Put Forth a Number of Theories and Speculations

John Pickett was no fool. Once he had recovered from the initial shock, he lost no time in wrapping his arms around the lady and returning her kiss with feeling. A faint gasp sounded from the open doorway, then the door closed with a faint click and the footsteps receded. Neither Pickett nor the viscountess, however, demonstrated any great eagerness to return to their search, but remained locked in a fervent embrace for a full thirty seconds after the hall had fallen silent. Alas, sanity eventually reasserted itself, and Lady Fieldhurst took a wobbly step backwards.

"I-I beg your pardon!" she stammered, blushing crimson. "I could think of no other way to account for our presence here, and at such an hour."

"Very—" The word came out on a squeak. He cleared his throat and tried again. "Very resourceful of you, my lady."

"Who was it? Did you see?" A lock of her hair had come loose and now caressed her shoulder. Irrelevantly, Pickett wondered if it had been dislodged by her removal of the hair pin, or by his own probing fingers.

"No. I—" *I had my eyes closed.* A fine admission for a Bow Street Runner to make! "—I couldn't tell."

She looked down at the open drawer. "Whoever it was, they're gone now. I daresay we can get on with it. The search, I mean," she added hastily.

Nodding agreement, he removed the drawer from its tracks

and set it on top of the desk. Lady Fieldhurst gathered up the loose papers on the top, while Pickett turned his attention to the ledger, starting at the back with the most recent entries and working his way forward.

"What a scrawl!" he muttered, moving his candle nearer in the vain hope that brighter illumination would somehow make Sir Gerald's penmanship more legible. "I don't know why he bothered to lock the thing up; no one else could make head or tail of it."

The viscountess, in the meantime, discovered that her pile of papers consisted mostly of correspondence. The majority of these had to do with Miss Hollingshead's approaching London season: there were numerous letters from estate agents quoting rates for hiring a house for the Season in a fashionable part of Town, and one confirming the date of Miss Hollingshead's presentation ball, along with a receipt for the deposit paid in advance for the hiring of suitable assembly rooms. In stark contrast to these were three letters from various clergymen, each recommending his protégé for the vacant vicarship. The contrast between Miss Hollingshead's desires and those of her parents could not have been more clearly demonstrated.

For his part, Pickett found nothing in the ledger that could be construed as blackmail payments. Indeed, the only transactions between Sir Gerald and Mr. Danvers were ones in which the vicar, not the baronet, was the recipient, and these were hardly sinister: a handsome donation toward restoring the medieval bell tower, and a number of smaller ones for various parish charities.

"If our man Danvers was being blackmailed by anyone, it wasn't Sir Gerald," Pickett concluded with a sigh as he closed the ledger.

"There is nothing here, either, except for the financial details of Miss Hollingshead's presentation," concurred the viscountess, laying aside the last of the letters. "In fact, the entire evening appears to have been a complete waste of time."

Pickett understood what she meant, but the remark stung all the same. Only moments ago, she had kissed him with great feeling. How could she dismiss the incident as a waste of time, when his entire world had just tilted on its axis?

Lady Fieldhurst lingered in bed the following morning, but her slothfulness was not entirely due to her nocturnal adventures. No, her reluctance to rise was more attributable to a pronounced dread at the prospect of putting in an appearance at breakfast, where her *faux* footman would no doubt be waiting to serve her. She did not know how she could look John Pickett in the face. She had not kissed a man since her husband was alive—and, if truth be told, it had been many years since she and the late Lord Fieldhurst had kissed with anything approaching the enthusiasm of last night's performance.

Seeing that she could delay the inevitable meeting no longer, she threw back the covers and set about making her daily ablutions. For all his youth, she reasoned, John Pickett was an intelligent man. He would surely understand that that kiss had been nothing more than an expedient solution to an unavoidable crisis—wouldn't he?

By the time she reached the breakfast room, the family had apparently already partaken, for the sunny chamber was empty save for a very tall young footman in blue and silver livery.

"Good morning, my lady," he said stiffly, holding out a chair for her.

"Good morning, John," she responded in kind, coloring slightly as she allowed him to seat her at the table.

"Coffee, my lady?" He had the mouth of a poet, a full lower lip supporting a perfect Cupid's bow above. Why had she never noticed?

"Chocolate, please."

As he filled a delicate Spode cup with steaming chocolate, she noted with relief (and, illogically, a slight feeling of annoyance) that there was nothing in either his bearing or the tone of his voice to suggest that he remembered the events of the previous night at all. She could not know what an effort his seeming indifference cost him. She was in the act of accepting the cup of chocolate from his hand when the door opened. Emma Hollingshead froze on the threshold.

"Oh, I beg your pardon!" she exclaimed, blushing furiously. "I was—that is, I thought perhaps my mother was here."

"I haven't seen Lady Anne this morning," said Lady Fieldhurst, puzzled by the young lady's obvious discomfort. "I supposed she had already breakfasted."

"Yes, I-I daresay you are right. Pray—pray forgive me for interrupting."

She ducked out of the room and quickly shut the door behind her.

"There's one mystery solved, at any rate," Pickett observed.

"Oh?" inquired her ladyship.

"We know now who opened the library door last night."

"Miss Hollingshead? Why do you say so?"

"Because," he said wryly, "only a gently bred young woman who had caught a houseguest and her servant in a passionate embrace could possibly look even guiltier than we do."

She was startled into looking him full in the face for the first time since entering the room, and his expression was so comically sheepish that she had to laugh. Her own expression must have mirrored his, for he laughed, too, and with that shared amusement, the earlier awkwardness fled.

"I wonder why she was up and about so late at night?" Pickett removed the cover from a silver chafing dish. "Something to do with Mr. Meriwether, I'll wager."

"Very likely. But what will you do next, now that you must acquit Sir Gerald? You can hardly go prowling about the countryside ransacking the neighbors' libraries and rummaging through their ledgers." She frowned in sudden suspicion. "*Can* you?"

"Alas, no," conceded Pickett. "I'll have to look for more indirect evidence. Did anyone present at dinner that night appear to have an urgent need for funds?"

"No, but then, this is not London," pointed out the viscountess. "One can live quite comfortably in the country on no more than two hundred pounds per annum."

Pickett, who had never possessed such a sum in his entire life, let this observation pass without comment.

"Does anyone appear to have come into a sum of money recently?"

"It is difficult to say, as I had no previous acquaintance with any of them except Lady Anne." Lady Fieldhurst considered the question for a long moment. "What about Robert Kendall?" she suggested at last.

"The dandy? I wouldn't have thought he had the brains to plot such a scheme."

"He is no intellectual, I grant you, but he is not without cunning. If you could but hear the barbs he throws at poor Mr. Meriwether—"

" '*Poor* Mr. Meriwether'?" quoted Pickett. "Do you mean that literally or figuratively?"

"Both, I daresay. But if you are picturing him in the rôle of blackmailer, pray think again! It is Mr. Danvers's position, not his purse, that Mr. Meriwether had reason to covet. If he had attempted blackmail, it would have been to coerce Mr. Danvers into an early retirement, and perhaps a recommendation to Sir Gerald that he—Mr. Meriwether, that is—be given the post."

"Whereas Mr. Kendall—?" prompted Pickett.

"Mr. Kendall favors a style of dress which is extremely expensive, and which his father despises. I can't see Lord Kendall giving his son an allowance that would enable him to indulge his deplorable tastes, can you?"

"Since I've never met the gentleman, I couldn't say," said Pickett, refilling her cup. "It sounds like a reasonable assumption, though. Anyone else?"

"What about Miss Grantham?"

"The governess? But you said she was potty on him!"

In fact, Pickett was not at all certain her ladyship was not roasting him again, but she answered him with every appearance of earnestness.

"It would not be the first time a man had been murdered by a woman who fancied herself in love with him," she pointed out with unarguable logic. "Suppose Miss Grantham finally realized that her ambitions in that direction were hopeless. In three years—four at the most—Miss Susannah will leave the schoolroom, and the Hollingsheads will have no further need of Miss Grantham's services. She will find it most difficult, at her age, to find a new position."

"Surely the Hollingsheads would offer her some sort of a pension," suggested Pickett.

"They may, of course, but they are under no obligation to do so. Perhaps, having witnessed their cavalier treatment of Mr. Meriwether, who has the supposed advantage of kinship, Miss Grantham could not feel sanguine about her own expectations."

"And so, having somehow discovered the skeleton in the vicarage cupboard, she sets about building herself a tidy little nest egg at her false lover's expense."

"Something like that. Only I suspect Mr. Danvers would be much shocked to hear himself described as Miss Grantham's lover, false or otherwise. He appears to have given her no encouragement at all—unless you consider his requesting her to read that massive tome of his as evidence of amorous intentions."

"No, but that raises another question: why would he make such a request of a woman who was blackmailing him?"

"Perhaps the demands for payment were arranged in such a way that he did not know his blackmailer's identity. Or," she added with mounting enthusiasm, "perhaps the request was not a request at all, but a form of clandestine communication."

"Pound notes slipped between the pages?"

"Yes, or a letter refusing payment and informing her that he intended to make a clean breast of the matter."

Pickett frowned. "It's possible, but it seems—I don't know, overly dramatic. Like something you might see on the stage at Drury Lane."

"My dear John, remember we are speaking of a spinster lady of advancing years and limited income. High drama would *not* be considered a disadvantage. In fact, I daresay she craves it almost as much as she does security—perhaps even more so."

"I can't say I like Miss Grantham as a blackmailer any more than I like her as a murderess, but I'll bear it in mind," Pickett promised. "Now, who else?"

Lady Fieldhurst sighed. "We are rapidly exhausting the possibilities. I can't imagine Lord Kendall in the rôle of blackmailer, as he is a Justice of the Peace—"

"A corrupt magistrate? Stranger things have happened, I assure you."

"—While as for Mr. Carrington, I fear I know very little about him. According to Mr. Meriwether, he has only lived in the area for a couple of years, so he is still a stranger by local standards."

"A couple of years," echoed Pickett. "That would put him arriving here at about the same time Will's adoptive parents died."

"I suppose so," said her ladyship, much struck. "Is there a connection?"

"I don't know—perhaps not. But I think I should visit Little Neddleby and poke around a bit."

The viscountess raised a hand to forestall the inevitable question. "And you will naturally need a day off for this excursion! Very well, you know I must grant it. But what, pray, are you looking for?"

"Anything I can find about Will's past and anyone who might have known about his true parentage. If I can find out who knew, I'll know who would have had the means for blackmail."

Lady Fieldhurst set her cup down on its saucer with a *clink* and made as if to rise from the table. "And while you are doing that, I shall see what I can discover about the mysterious Mr. Carrington."

Pickett, finding himself shirking his duty, moved quickly to hold her chair for her. "How will you do that?"

"I have an excellent idea," declared her ladyship, smiling mischievously up at him. "We widows are so very lonely, you know, and it is such a comfort to have a man to whom we may turn for companionship."

"I *hate* that idea," Pickett muttered to her retreating back.

Immediately upon exiting the breakfast room, Lady Fieldhurst was appalled at her own audacity. What had possessed her to volunteer to play the coquette for a veritable stranger in whom she had not the slightest amorous interest? Surely, she told herself firmly, it was the duty of every citizen to see criminals brought to justice. Therefore, she was doing no more than her duty in helping further Bow Street's investigations. It had nothing at all to do with the fact that Bow Street had kissed her passionately the previous evening (for although a strict interpretation of the evening's events must insist that *she* had kissed *him*, there was no denying the fact that he had most certainly kissed her back) only to leave her alone with a murderer in the vicinity. Very well, then, she would obtain what information she could from the gentleman in question, and if John Pickett should return from his wanderings to discover that she had been foully done to death, it would be no more than he deserved.

Having resigned herself to perform her duty as an Englishwoman, Lady Fieldhurst set out to locate Lady Anne in order to gently press her hostess into setting a date for one of the proposed sightseeing expeditions. While the viscountess was prepared to flirt with any number of gentlemen for a sufficiently worthy cause, she found the prospect of doing so at Hollingshead Place, where John Pickett might be hovering within earshot at any given moment, daunting in the extreme.

She had not far to look for Lady Anne, for as she neared the drawing room, she heard that lady's voice itemizing the details of Miss Hollingshead's approaching Season, to which Emma returned monosyllabic replies.

"—Your presentation at Court, of course, and my brother, your uncle Lord Claridge, has promised to host a dinner in your honor that evening. Ah, my dear Lady Fieldhurst," she said, looking up at the viscountess's entrance, "I wonder if you might spare your John to us this morning? The plans for Emma's Season, you must know, are proceeding apace, and I wish to have him measured for a suit of Hollingshead livery."

"Mama—"

However out of favor John Pickett might be at the moment, the thought of him clad in the scarlet and gold of the Hollingshead servants was too repugnant for Lady Fieldhurst to contemplate. "Oh! You—you have spoken to him, then?"

"Mama, I don't think—"

"I have not broached the subject with him yet," admitted Lady Anne. "I can see by your face that you think me a trifle premature, but I know young people and, if you will forgive my saying so, no matter how loyal he may be to your interests, it would be a very unusual young person who would prefer the sobriety of a house of mourning to the gaieties of the London Season."

"Mama, I don't think you should attempt to hire Lady Fieldhurst's footman away!"

Lady Anne blinked at the vehemence of her daughter's protest. "Good heavens, why not? Should he choose to leave her services, I will of course see that she is well compensated for the loss."

"You don't understand," Emma Hollingshead continued. "He is—they are—oh!" With a little cry of embarrassed frustration, she fled the room.

"What do you suppose has come over the girl?" her fond parent wondered aloud.

The moment of reckoning, it appeared, was at hand. Lady Fieldhurst took a deep breath. There was no need for her to feel embarrassed, no need at all. This was, after all, precisely what she had wished the midnight visitor to believe, in the hopes of covering up more sinister motives. "I fear I am to blame, ma'am. Mr. Danvers's tragic—accident—has affected me very deeply, coming so soon after my own husband's untimely death. My footman is aware of my distress, and was attempting to—console me—when your daughter surprised us in the library."

"I see," said Lady Anne. "I need not ask, of course, what form this consolation takes. I daresay I should have surmised as much when I learned you had sent for him. However little I may condone such unions, I would not presume to dictate to a guest. I must insist, however, that any such liaisons conducted beneath my roof be carried out with the utmost discretion. My daughter already has a number of foolish ideas about love and romance without filling her head with notions of a grand passion belowstairs."

For one brief moment Lady Fieldhurst wondered if her

hostess's interest in hiring Pickett sprang from similarly carnal motives but rejected the notion as absurd; however susceptible that lady's daughters might be to the tender passion (and Susannah clearly was not immune to Pickett's charm), the viscountess could not imagine Lady Anne indulging in any amorous activity beyond closing her eyes and thinking of England.

"Of course. I deeply regret the incident, for I would not wish to give Miss Hollingshead false ideas of what to expect once she is married. I daresay I should have returned to London as soon as I, er, felt the need for John's companionship," Lady Fieldhurst continued disingenuously, "but I confess to a reluctance to leave Yorkshire without having first explored the beauties of the countryside. What a pity the weather has been so uncooperative! I always feel one cannot truly claim to have spent a holiday in the country until one has scrambled over the stones of at least one picturesque ruin."

The effects of this gentle hint were all that the viscountess might have wished.

"I fear your entertainment has been shockingly neglected," confessed Lady Anne, once more the gracious hostess. "I am at fault in keeping you tied to the house, for in spite of your widowed state, you are nearer my daughter's age than my own, and no doubt thirst for some novel form of amusement. You must allow me to make it up to you."

Lady Fieldhurst instantly demurred, but her hostess insisted, just as the viscountess had known she would. By the time Lady Fieldhurst returned to her room that evening to dress for dinner, she was able to inform Pickett that he might have his day off; she would have no need of his services the following day, as she was to accompany a party of pleasure-seekers to Knaresborough to explore Mother Shipton's Cave.

Chapter 9

Which Finds John Pickett Trudging About the Countryside

John Pickett awoke at dawn and rolled over in bed with a groan. He'd had twenty-four hours in which to wallow in the memory of Lady Fieldhurst's kiss; now it was time to get back to the business which had brought him to Yorkshire in the first place. As he threw back the bedclothes, however, he could not shake the feeling that he was chasing after mares' nests. He had no real proof that the vicar was being blackmailed at all and no reason to suppose that a visit to Little Neddleby would reveal the identity of the blackmailer even if such a person existed. No, his time would be far better spent accompanying her ladyship to Knaresborough and seeing that the male contingent, particularly the enigmatic Mr. Jasper Carrington, kept a respectful distance.

So that was it, was it? Muttering something under his breath about a dog in the manger, he sat up and reached for his breeches. He had best away to Little Neddleby with all possible speed; the sooner he solved this case and returned to Bow Street, the better off he would be.

The familiar feel of his comfortable brown serge coat and gloriously unpowdered hair did much to improve his outlook, and his spirits were further lifted when he entered the servants' dining hall to find Mrs. Holland descending upon him with the light of battle in her eyes. It was, he reflected, truly amazing what one kiss could do for a man's confidence, even when the kiss was prompted by expedience rather than affection.

"And where, pray, do you think you're going, dressed like that?" the housekeeper demanded, waving a contemptuous hand at his unliveried person.

He met her outraged look with one of limpid innocence. "To Little Neddleby, ma'am."

"Little Neddleby?" Mrs. Holland's formidable bosom swelled with outrage, at considerable risk to her starched black bodice. "And what would her ladyship say to that, I wonder?"

Pickett regarded her with mild surprise. "I doubt her ladyship would find much in Little Neddleby to interest her."

The housekeeper's beady eyes narrowed in suspicion. "Tell me, does her ladyship know about this little sojourn of yours?"

"Oh, yes!" Pickett assured her. "I told her ladyship I needed the day off, and she said I might have it."

"You told her—?" Words failing her, Mrs. Holland sputtered for a moment before continuing, "You've a sight too much cheek for your own good, you have! At the rate you're going, you won't be long in her ladyship's service, you mark my words!"

"You're probably right," said Pickett.

The unexpectedly wistful note in his voice startled her into silence.

Pickett had just taken his seat at the breakfast table when Molly sidled up to him and sat down much too close. "I hear you're going to Little Neddleby," she breathed into his ear. "Care for some company?"

In fact, there was nothing Pickett would like less. "Thank you, but I shouldn't like to take you away from your duties here."

"No fear of that, for 'tis my half-day." Beneath the table, her foot curled around his ankle. "Just say the word, and I can be ready in a trice."

"I'm afraid you would be bored," Pickett said resolutely. "It won't be a pleasure jaunt."

"I don't know about that," purred Molly. "You might be surprised." Her fingers closed around his knee and began to work their way upward.

Pickett leaped up from the table so quickly that his chair tumbled over behind him. "I shouldn't want to be late," he said, and made his escape.

Molly gave a little huff. "*Some* people wouldn't know what to do with a woman if one bit 'em on the arse," she muttered, and turned her attention to the more receptive second footman.

After his abortive breakfast, Pickett set out for the village, from which point he hoped to board a stage for Little Neddleby. His determination to focus his attention on the case at hand suffered a setback as he approached the river, for it was here where the damp ground sloped down to the water that Lady Fieldhurst had slipped and had clung to his arm for support. And here, as they had crossed the bridge, she had tucked her hand through the crook of his elbow.

And here, he reminded himself sternly, Mr. Danvers lay in a fresh grave while his killer walked free. With renewed determination, he thrust the viscountess resolutely to the back of his mind and climbed the sloping path leading into the village.

Pickett, born and bred in one of the largest cities in the world, was no great lover of the country. Indeed, there were occasions, such as the one which presented itself on that particular morning, when he heartily despised it. For upon reaching the Pig and Whistle and inquiring of the proprietor as to the next stage for Little Neddleby, he was met with an indulgent laugh and a wholly unacceptable answer.

"Lord love you, lad, there's no stage what stops at Little Neddleby," said this worthy. "You'll have to walk. It's naught but nine miles—five, as the crow flies."

"No stage at all?" pressed Pickett, hoping to be contradicted. "It needn't be the Royal Mail."

"None at all," his informer confirmed. "Oh, you could ride straight through and get off at Otley, but you'd have to walk back almost half as far again."

By this time Pickett's plight had attracted the attention of the three other occupants of the tap room, all country folk who felt it incumbent upon them to offer him the benefit of their advice.

"This is Tuesday, ain't it?" asked one. "Old Mrs. Fleer always brings her butter and eggs to the village of a Tuesday. You could always ride back to Little Neddleby with her, provided you've no objection to riding in a farm wagon."

Having no such scruples, Pickett would have leaped at this offer, but before he could inquire further as to Mrs. Fleer's current whereabouts, the tapster vetoed this promising suggestion.

"Not today she ain't, for 'tain't a market day. Mrs. Fleer only comes to the village on market day."

This observation led, in the time-honored tradition of country people, to a lengthy and spirited discussion of the habits of Mrs. Fleer, her husband, and various other persons in whom Pickett had not the slightest interest. By the time his advisers had agreed that he was unlikely to find anyone headed for Little Neddleby until later in the week, they were surprised (and somewhat offended) to discover that they had lost their audience; Pickett had long since set out for Little Neddleby on foot.

He reached his destination some three hours later, having been obliged, owing to unfamiliarity with the area, to keep to the main road. Upon entering the village, he stopped in the local public house for both information and liquid refreshment. As the publican set before him a tankard of foaming ale, Pickett made a few trite observations about the weather, to which the man behind the bar responded in expansive fashion. Having soon exhausted this topic—and, more to the point, established good relations with his host—Pickett broached the subject which was the object of his visit.

"You must do a lively business on a day as warm as this," he observed with perhaps more optimism than accuracy.

"Aye, that I do," the barkeep boasted. "I'll wager there's not a man in the village who don't wet his whistle at the Cock and Bull at least two or three times in a se'ennight."

"Is that so?" asked Pickett admiringly. "You must know everyone in the village, then."

"Aye, and their wives and children, too," agreed mine host, holding no truck with false modesty.

"Know of anyone by the name of Huggins?"

"Huggins," echoed the publican, frowning in concentration.

"Man and wife," Pickett prompted. "I believe they had a boy by the name of Will."

"Ah, Huggins!" exclaimed the publican as light dawned. "They died, both of 'em, oh, two years ago."

Pickett nodded. "That's the pair."

"Sad business, that. The boy took off right after they was buried and hasn't been seen nor heard from since." He shook his head. "And after they'd loved him and raised him like he was their own."

"The boy was a foster child, then?"

"Oh, aye." The publican leaned across the bar and lowered his voice to a conspiratorial whisper. "By-blow of a churchman, or so they say."

"No!" Pickett breathed, leaning closer.

"As I live and breathe," declared his host. "Rector of the next parish but one. Rode up one day with the babe and left him with the Hugginses. Mrs. Huggins was that happy to have the lad, too, she having just lost a babe of her own."

"Who was the woman? The child's mother?"

"Now, that's just what I don't know, nor does anyone else that I ever heard. She might have been a foreigner, or else a gypsy, for the lad's as black as a burned stump."

Having recently seen Will Huggins in close proximity to a burned stump (or a reasonable facsimile thereof), Pickett knew this for an exaggeration. Still, the coincidence of Will's having joined the gypsies after the death of his foster parents was too striking to ignore. Further questioning yielded the information that no strangers (barring Pickett himself, of course) had been to Little Neddleby making inquiries about the Hugginses or their adoptive son. So helpful, in fact, was the publican that when Pickett expressed interest in seeing the Huggins cottage for himself, that worthy felt duty bound to advise him against what was bound to be a wasted effort. But Pickett was insistent nevertheless, and so in the end the barkeep was obliged to furnish his guest with directions.

"But there's nothing there no more, not with the folks dead and the boy gone," he added by way of a parting shot.

Pickett understood this caveat to be figurative, that the publican had meant that he would find nothing of value in the vacant cottage, nothing that might assist him in his quest. When he reached the place the publican had described, however, he discovered the man's words to be quite literal: there was nothing there, unless one cared to count a lone chimney rising from the ground like an obelisk. At its base, long grasses had forced their way through tumbled stones and now waved in the light breeze. With a sinking heart, Pickett stepped over the stones into what had once been a home, and kicked at the ground with the toe of his boot. Beneath the grass was a layer of white ash and blackened splinters of wood that disintegrated underfoot.

Ashes to ashes, dust to dust . . .

Within the next year or two, the vicarage at Hollingshead would no doubt look equally abandoned, having recently met with a similar fate. For at some point in the not too distant past, the Huggins cottage had burned to the ground.

Chapter 10

Which Finds Lady Fieldhurst at Mother Shipton's Cave

While Pickett trudged up the road toward Little Neddleby, Lady Fieldhurst partook of an early breakfast with the Hollingshead family. It was not a particularly pleasant meal; Lady Anne and her daughter had apparently quarreled again—presumably over that young lady's attachment to Mr. Meriwether, conspicuous of late by his very absence. At present, Lady Anne's cool courtesy and her daughter's red-rimmed eyes made Lady Fieldhurst think longingly of the days of unrelieved boredom so confidently predicted weeks earlier by her friend Emily. Only Sir Gerald, fortifying himself for a day's fishing, appeared unmoved by the strained atmosphere prevailing at the breakfast table.

A welcome interruption occurred in the arrival of Miss Susannah, accompanied by her governess. Unlike her elder sister, that damsel was in fine fettle, as she was not only being spared the thin porridge which comprised the usual schoolroom fare, but also being granted the unparalleled privilege of joining the expedition to Mother Shipton's Cave. The one obstacle to her happiness was the presence of Miss Grantham, who seemed determined to destroy her pleasure in the outing by turning it into an educational experience.

"Be sure to bring your sketchbook and pencils," the governess reminded her pupil. "Besides the cave itself, we must take particular note of the Petrifying Well nearby."

"Is it true," demanded Miss Susannah, slathering marmalade

over her toast, "that objects placed within the Petrifying Well soon turn to stone?"

"No, it is most certainly not true," replied Miss Grantham sternly. "They do not 'turn to stone' at all. They become encased in limestone."

Miss Susannah continued undaunted, "May I bring something to place there? I have a handkerchief." She produced a square of inexpertly embroidered linen from her pocket. "May I leave it there and see if it will turn to stone?"

"May I leave it there and see if it will *become encased in limestone.*"

"I beg your pardon, Miss Grantham." Surveying her handiwork with a critical eye, Susannah picked at a loose thread. "May I, please?"

Miss Grantham regarded the uneven stitches with a pained expression. "Yes, you may. Unfortunately, your needlework appears to be suited for very little else."

Having achieved this ambition, Miss Susannah turned her attention to the viscountess. "Where is John this morning, Lady Fieldhurst?" she inquired with transparent eagerness. "Does he mean to accompany us?"

Seeing Lady Anne frowning over the rim of her coffee cup, Lady Fieldhurst felt her face grow warm. "I'm afraid not. John has the day off."

Although her obligation to her hostess demanded that she not encourage the girl in an inappropriate attachment, Lady Fieldhurst could not suppress a sympathetic smile at Miss Susannah's crestfallen expression. Indeed, she was conscious of a similar depression of her own spirits when she thought of Pickett's protracted absence.

"I am sure it will be his loss," Lady Fieldhurst said dismissively, then turned to her hostess. "But where is Philip? Is he not to join us?"

"My son is indisposed this morning, and sends his regrets."

In fact, Philip Hollingshead's "regrets" consisted of hurling a pillow at the servant sent to awaken him, then clutching his aching head and demanding to be left alone. Lady Fieldhurst had no way of knowing this, but in view of John Pickett's revelations concerning that young man, she quite correctly ascribed his indisposition to the aftereffects of drinking too much alcohol.

"And what of you, Sir Gerald?" she asked her host. "I should have thought an outdoorsman such as yourself would not want to miss such an expedition. Surely the local trout population will keep for another day."

"Oh, I've seen Mother Shipton's Cave a thousand times," declared Sir Gerald around a mouthful of buttered eggs. "Got lost in it once when I was a boy. You'd best have a care, Sukey, and make sure you don't go that same road," he cautioned his youngest child.

"I am sure Miss Grantham will take excellent care of her," put in Lady Anne.

"Indeed, Miss Susannah will be in no danger, for we shall sit on the grass and sketch," Miss Grantham said primly. "I cannot think it proper for a young girl to go gadding about inside a cave."

Seeing Miss Susannah open her mouth to protest this injustice, Lady Fieldhurst quickly came to her defense before that damsel could disgrace herself. "Oh, pray let her explore the cave! Indeed, you should do so as well. I am sure you must be sorely in need of diversion, so occupied as you have been recently with Mr. Danvers's book."

"Eh? What's this?" inquired Sir Gerald jovially. "Are we never to hear the end of that blasted book?"

"Poor Mr. Danvers asked me to read his manuscript for errors," Miss Grantham explained. She dabbed at her eyes with a corner of her serviette. "Those were among the last words he ever spoke to me."

Emma Hollingshead, seated beside the governess, patted her hand consolingly, but Lady Anne ignored this display of sensibility on the part of her employee. "I would accompany you myself," she said, "were I not obliged to pay calls of charity on the parish poor. Not, I fear, a pleasant task, but such an important one, especially now that we are without a vicar. I should have thought the curate would perform this particular duty, but it appears he is more interested in larking about in pursuit of pleasure."

Miss Hollingshead turned quite pink in the face. "How can you say so, Mama, when it was you who invited him to accompany us?"

"Since Mr. Meriwether is our distant cousin, Emma, I could hardly exclude one of the Family," said her mother in quelling accents. "However, he was under no such obligation to accept the invitation once it was offered. His disregard for the needs of the parish makes me question his readiness for such a responsibility."

"Yes, Mama," Miss Hollingshead said woodenly, sipping her chocolate. But although her eyes were meekly downcast, her knuckles shone white on the elegantly curved handle of her cup.

The group rose from the breakfast table just as the butler entered the room with the information that the other merrymakers had arrived. After a general exchange of greetings all around, Lady Anne took charge of dividing the party into three smaller groups, more or less equally distributed among the three available conveyances.

"Cousin Colin, will you be so good as to escort my daughter and her governess?" she asked Mr. Meriwether, gesturing with one white hand toward the cumbersome Hollingshead carriage.

"I should be honored," the curate assured her with every indication of sincerity. However, Lady Fieldhurst could not help noticing the light that flared briefly in his eyes only to be extinguished when the mention of Miss Grantham made it plain to him precisely which of Lady Anne's daughters he was to accompany. Was Lady Anne truly so oblivious to the young man's disappointment, the viscountess wondered, or did she take a certain cruel satisfaction in dashing his hopes?

"Mr. Kendall, we must not allow Lady Fieldhurst to return to London without having been tooled about in your new phaeton," Lady Anne continued, giving her elder daughter an almost imperceptible nudge toward the only gentleman of the party who did not consider himself a suitor for her hand. "Mr. Carrington, if you would be so kind as to take Emma up in your curricle?"

The three gentlemen moved toward the various carriages in order to assist their fair passengers, and Lady Fieldhurst realized that the time for her performance was at hand. She gave a surreptitious tug to the neckline of her gray walking dress, reminding herself that she was, at least for the nonce, a merry widow engaged in an amorous intrigue with her footman and open to the prospect of a second intrigue with a gentleman of her own class. Thrusting her shoulders back in order to make the most of an admittedly small bosom, she edged away from Robert Kendall's dashing vehicle and sidled nearer to Mr. Carrington and his more sedate equipage.

"Oh, my!" she exclaimed, clasping one gloved hand to her bosom. "I am quite terrified, Mr. Kendall. Such great yellow wheels! Why, I daresay we shall be sitting at least four feet off the ground!"

"Five," he confessed with a smug smile.

"*Five?* Worse and worse! Mr. Carrington, if I fall out of Mr. Kendall's phaeton, you must promise to come at once to my rescue."

Jasper Carrington did not disappoint. "I confess, I cannot

feel quite safe in these high-perch jobs myself. If you would prefer to take a seat in my curricle—"

"I say, what a capital notion!" seconded Mr. Kendall with unflattering eagerness. "You will be much more comfortable with Mr. Carrington, and Emma—Miss Hollingshead—may ride with me."

This proposal being agreed upon by all parties, it was quickly put into practice. Lady Fieldhurst allowed Mr. Carrington to hand her up into his curricle, then smiled coyly down at him.

"What an excellent carriage this is! I shall feel quite safe now," she said, patting the seat invitingly.

He climbed up beside her, and soon they were bowling along at a smart pace with Mr. Kendall's phaeton before them and the Hollingshead berline bringing up the rear. The sun had by this time grown quite warm, and Lady Fieldhurst unfurled a dove-gray sunshade adorned with black ribbons.

"How thankful I am to be in Yorkshire and not London!" she declared to her traveling companion. "I shudder to think of what the Metropolis must be like in such weather." She suited the word to the deed, shrugging her shoulders in a way that made her bodice inch still lower.

"You should be thankful, then, that we are in England and not in India."

While courteous enough, this tepid response to her unsubtle invitation suggested a most unflattering immunity to her charms. Still, Mr. Carrington had given her a golden opportunity to turn the conversation, and she did not hesitate to make the most of it.

"Were you very long in India, then?"

He inclined his head in acknowledgement. "Twenty years with the East India Company. In fact, it was in India that I first made the acquaintance of Mr. Danvers."

"Did you, indeed?" asked Lady Fieldhurst, squirreling away

this information for the future edification of John Pickett. "What a surprise it must have been for you, to discover that your acquaintance from the East was now your near neighbor!"

"Oh, it was no surprise. I knew he had taken up a position as rector of this parish. In fact, it was for that reason that I decided to settle here."

"The two of you must have been very close," observed the viscountess.

"Close?" Mr. Carrington shook his head. "I fear our personalities differed too much for intimacy. I was a rackety young man come East to make my fortune, and he was a missionary to the natives."

"A noble calling."

"Indeed it was, and it would have been difficult to find a man better suited to it. I believe he might have been happy to remain there for the rest of his life, had not his health necessitated his removal to a more moderate climate."

His health, Lady Fieldhurst wondered, or his reputation? She had never seen the vicar's illegitimate son, but if John Pickett were to be believed, the boy was as dark as a gypsy—or, perhaps, as a Hindoo. But if the missionary had fathered a son on one of the native women, surely it would have been safer to have left the child in India, rather than risk the scandal following him back to England.

Realizing that some response was expected of her, Lady Fieldhurst hurried into speech.

"And so Mr. Danvers returned to England for his health, only to meet with a vi—" She had almost said "violent," then remembered that none of his neighbors realized the vicar had been murdered. "—Tragic death," she amended hastily. "Life is full of ironies, is it not? But do not let us talk of such things on such a glorious day! Pray, tell me more of India! Are the women there very beautiful?"

"Oh, *very* beautiful," he assured her. "Though of course they can't hold a candle to our English ladies."

"Very prettily said, sir," applauded the viscountess. "And yet England's beauties failed to tempt either you or Mr. Danvers to matrimony."

"Ah, but marriage is a very different thing," Mr. Carrington observed with a roguish smile.

Lady Fieldhurst laughed coquettishly, but in spite of her best efforts to draw him out, her companion never confided the least hint of romantic intrigue on the vicar's part. If Mr. Carrington knew anything about Mr. Danvers's indiscretions (which by this time she had begun to doubt) he clearly intended that the vicar's secrets should die with him.

Satisfied (albeit disappointed) that she would get no more pertinent information from Mr. Carrington, she resolved to focus her efforts on Mr. Kendall. But when the party stopped in Knaresborough for a light luncheon, it was borne in upon her that she would have a rival for that young man's attentions. At any other time, she might have found it amusing to watch Miss Hollingshead flirting outrageously with the young dandy while ignoring her once-favored suitor. At the moment, however, this obstacle to her plans left the viscountess feeling almost as frustrated as the despondent curate. Her position at the table precluded conversation, sandwiched as she was between the gallant but unforthcoming Mr. Carrington on her right, and the garrulous Miss Susannah on her left. Eventually their meal was completed and the party piled back into their various vehicles, but here, too, her efforts were thwarted, hoist, as it were, on her own petard: she could hardly ask Mr. Kendall to take her up in his phaeton now, after perjuriously professing herself terrified of it.

At last the three vehicles lurched to a stop and their passengers disembarked, all save Miss Susannah rather stiff from the drive. The ensuing walk through a stand of beeches, while hard on Lady Fieldhurst's new kid half boots, served to work out the soreness. By the time they reached the cave where Ursula Sontheil Shipton, renowned locally as a prophetess, had reputedly been born over three hundred years earlier, all seven were eager to explore the wonders of nature.

As they approached the Petrifying Well, Lady Fieldhurst saw her opportunity. Supposing that the six-and-twenty years in her dish would seem ancient to one only recently emancipated from Oxford, she abandoned the coquettish demeanor she had employed with Mr. Carrington, and instead drew from the example set by a number of dowagers who had terrified her during her first Season: expressing a wholly imaginary dread of turning her ankle on the uneven ground, she commandeered Mr. Robert Kendall's escort. That foppish young man was not proof against a determined lady, and so with one darkling glance at Emma Hollingshead approaching the well on Mr. Carrington's arm, he offered the viscountess his own. They exchanged polite commonplaces as they approached the sheer rock wall. Water cascaded over its face in a solid sheet, its flow interrupted at the base of the rock by various personal items—a glove here, a handkerchief there—in various stages of petrifaction. Miss Susannah, escaping from her governess, almost fell into the water in her eagerness to add her own contribution to the collection.

"What an excellent notion!" exclaimed the viscountess, and began to tug at the fingers of her black leather gloves.

"Here, no need for that," protested Robert Kendall feebly, tugging off his own York tan glove with obviously reluctant chivalry. "Allow me."

"Oh, but I insist, Mr. Kendall," said Lady Fieldhurst with her most charming smile. "I am wearied to death with black gloves and welcome the opportunity to rid myself of them, if only for a little while. You can have no notion of how tiresome it is, being obliged to subjugate one's own taste to others' notions of what is proper."

A disinterested observer might have pointed out that her walking dress, though sober in hue, was nevertheless in the first stare of fashion. Young Mr. Kendall, however, was far from disinterested. In fact, he was much struck by the hitherto unsuspected similarity in their respective situations.

"Say no more, my lady!" he exclaimed, regarding with new eyes this unexpected soulmate. "I know exactly how you feel! Although I am not in mourning, as you are, I have frequently been obliged to set aside some modish new garment because of my father's antiquated notions of what constitutes appropriate attire."

"How very distressing for you," commiserated her ladyship. "Every feeling revolts at such unnatural restrictions! Of course, I must consider myself fortunate in that I am at least financially independent of those members of my late husband's family who might seek to keep me in perpetual mourning, had they the power to do so. Others, I daresay, are not so fortunate," she added with eyes demurely downcast.

"I suppose I must consider myself fortunate in that regard as well," Mr. Kendall conceded grudgingly. "A modest competence from my godmother frees me from my father's purse strings, if not his tastes."

And so, thought Lady Fieldhurst, filing this information away for Pickett's consideration, Mr. Kendall had no shortage of funds and therefore no reason to blackmail Mr. Danvers.

The oddities of the Petrifying Well having been exhausted, the group turned their attention to the nearby cave. Avowing their determination to remain together, the intrepid explorers armed themselves with lanterns thoughtfully provided by Mr. Carrington. To the satisfaction of the entire party, even Miss

Grantham had apparently abandoned her intention of remaining outside, for she accepted a lantern willingly enough and led her enthusiastic young pupil into the darkness.

In spite of their stated intentions, it was perhaps inevitable that as they wandered deeper into the cave, whether by accident or design, the party split apart. First Miss Grantham and her charge stopped to examine a peculiar rock formation, then Mr. Kendall fell behind in order to remove a stone lodged in the heel of his boot. Lady Fieldhurst did not realize how isolated she had become, until she turned to address a remark to the curate, and found herself quite alone.

"Mr. Meriwether? Where are you?" The rock walls flung the question mockingly back at her.

"Mr. Meriwether?" she called again. "Mr. Carrington? Mr. Kendall?"

She held her lantern higher, but the meager flame failed to penetrate the inky blackness. Sir Gerald's boyhood recollections of being lost in the cave flooded her brain with vivid clarity. Clearly it behooved her to locate the rest of the party without delay. Unfortunately, she had no very clear idea of which direction to go. She turned and, choosing her steps with care, began to retrace her path. Air currents from unseen crevices caused the flame from her candle to dip and sway, and for one terrifying instant threatened to extinguish it altogether. At last, the sound of voices reached her ears. Picking up her pace, she moved in the direction from which they seemed to come. As she drew nearer, she recognized the voice as that of the curate, Mr. Meriwether.

"Will you not even speak to me? What have I done to give you such a disgust of me? Surely you must know that my feelings for you have not changed!"

"It is not your feelings that disgust me, but your actions!" Lady Fieldhurst was not surprised to learn that his companion was none other than Miss Hollingshead.

"My actions? Of what are you accusing me, Emma?"

"Where did you go when you left me that night? You could not have returned to your rooms in the village, for the bridge was out. So I ask again—where did you go?"

The simple question was followed by a silence which spoke volumes. For a long moment, there was no sound except the distant gurgling of a subterranean stream.

"You are quite right, Emma; I did not return to my rooms. I did not yet know the bridge was out, but I did not fancy slogging home through the mud. In fact, I had hoped to bed down in the stable for the night and resume my journey in the morning."

"The *stable?*" Emma Hollingshead's tone mingled amazement with skepticism. "Could you not have asked Mama to put you up for the night?"

"I daresay I could have, and I don't doubt she would have agreed to do so. You will no doubt think me proud to a fault, but I could not stomach the idea of casting myself on your mother's charity. Your father's groom, though a gruff sort of fellow, is a kindly soul who would not have objected." He paused, then spoke again with a hint of amusement in his voice. "You need not look so appalled, my love. If a stable was good enough for the Christ Child, it must surely have sufficed for me."

"No, no, it's just that—Colin, can you honestly tell me you were in the stable the entire time?"

"Until I returned to the house to beg a blanket from Mrs. Holland, only to learn that the vicarage was ablaze. Why do you ask?" She did not answer, and when he spoke again, his tone was grave. "If you fear that I might have seen or heard something I shouldn't, you need not worry, for you must know I could never betray you. I daresay you must have acted out of desperation, and dread of being forced into a hateful marriage.

For putting you in such a position, your mother must be held as much to blame as yourself."

"Good God, Colin, what are you suggesting? Can it be that you think me capable of—of—"

"We are all of us capable of the darkest deeds, Emma. History teaches us that, of all things."

"And why, pray, would I commit such a wicked act?"

"For love." The tenderness in his voice almost brought tears to Lady Fieldhurst's eyes. "For love of a man who can never marry you."

"But I didn't do it! You must know that I did not. In fact, I thought—I feared—You cannot deny that you had reason to wish him dead!"

"A man I loved like a father? No, Emma, I am sorry, but much as I love you, I confess I should be extremely reluctant to murder for your sake."

"But you said you had a plan that would allow us to marry," she reminded him.

"And so I did. I planned to write to one of my old schoolfellows who now has a modest living within his gift, and see if he would be willing to give it to me. The income is by no means large, but it would allow me to support a wife and, if we should be so blessed, a child or two."

"Oh, is that all it was?" breathed Emma on a sigh of relief. "I daresay you think me very foolish."

"Shall I tell you what I think of you, my dearest love?"

There followed a silence so very protracted that the viscountess began to despair of ever escaping from the cave at all. At length, weary of shifting her weight from one foot to another, she began to grope along the cave wall for a place to sit. A loose pebble shifted beneath her foot, skittering away in the darkness. A faint gasp sounded.

"My darling, we must not!" cried Miss Hollingshead.

"Someone is coming!"

Lady Fieldhurst seized her opportunity. Emerging from her hiding place with as much noise as she could contrive, she advanced upon the pair with loud exclamations of relief.

"Oh, Mr. Meriwether! Miss Hollingshead!" she cried, determinedly ignoring Miss Hollingshead's disheveled hair and the curate's rumpled cravat. "I somehow became separated from my companions and could not find my way back. I can never thank you enough for coming in search of me!"

Having provided the grateful pair with an excuse for their protracted absence, Lady Fieldhurst submitted with a good grace to their concerned (if somewhat belated) inquiries as to her health, safety, and state of mind. She took the arm Mr. Meriwether offered and allowed him to lead her out of the cave and into the sunshine. Other members of the party soon emerged from the inky depths, to be regaled with the story of Lady Fieldhurst's adventure (which, in the manner of such tales, grew more dramatic with each retelling) until at last the entire group was reunited.

"My dear Lady Fieldhurst!" exclaimed Miss Grantham, having been made privy by the now-thrilling tale. "You must be sorely in need of a restorative. I believe Mrs. Holland added a bottle of her special raspberry cordial to our picnic hamper. It is very good, I assure you."

Lady Fieldhurst, recalling that the picnic hamper was stored in the boot of the Hollingshead carriage, professed herself all eagerness for a draught of the housekeeper's raspberry cordial. In fact, she was less interested in a restorative than in cutting short the excursion and reporting her findings to John Pickett.

"So soon?" protested Miss Susannah, instructed to gather her sketchbook and follow her governess back to the carriage. "But I want to see if my handkerchief has been turned to stone!"

"I fear you would be disappointed," said Mr. Carrington with an indulgent smile. "The process of petrifaction takes several weeks. Perhaps we can manage a return visit at a later date."

With this vague promise Miss Susannah had to be content, and so the party trudged back through the beeches to the carriages. Their appetites sharpened through exercise, they made a hearty meal of cold chicken, bread, cheese, and apples from the Hollingshead orchard. At last, appetites sated, the little party broke up once more. Mr. Kendall, having extolled the virtues of his new phaeton, dragged Mr. Carrington on an inspection of this paragon among vehicles, while Mr. Meriwether and Miss Hollingshead wandered off and soon lost themselves among the beeches. Miss Grantham, having partaken a little too freely of Mrs. Holland's excellent cordial, dozed in the shade. Lady Fieldhurst, finding herself alone with Miss Susannah, knelt down on the grass near the spot where that young lady sat sketching.

"Miss Grantham appears to be sleeping soundly," observed the viscountess in a conspiratorial whisper. "I daresay you can stop drawing now, if you wish."

"Oh, I don't mind," said Miss Susannah, as her charcoal flew across the page.

"I fear I was never very artistic, myself," confessed her ladyship. "May I see your work?"

Miss Susannah hesitated only for a moment, then held out her sketchbook for the viscountess's inspection.

The face that gazed up at her from the page was instantly recognizable. The young artist had missed the nose entirely, and the eyes were a bit too close together, but the chin was his to the life, as was the mouth—the mouth that she herself had kissed scarcely more than twenty-four hours earlier.

"I tried to straighten his nose," confessed Miss Susannah, surveying her work critically, "but I think I prefer it the way it is."

Lady Fieldhurst was inclined to agree. Still, it was a remarkable effort for one so young, and the viscountess did not hesitate to give credit where it was due.

"It is very like," she told the budding artist. "You have quite a gift."

"Thank you. Miss Grantham only wants me to draw flowers and trees and such, but I think people are much more interesting, don't you?"

Lady Fieldhurst agreed, but privately she feared Miss Susannah found her most recent subject a great deal *too* interesting.

"I dare not keep it, for Miss Grantham would be furious if she saw it," said the artist with a sigh. "Do you think he might like to have it?"

Lady Fieldhurst had no difficulty interpreting "he" as the subject of the sketch. Recalling his dismay when informed of Miss Susannah's schoolgirl *tendre,* the viscountess could not quite suppress a mischievous smile. "I daresay he would like that very much." *And how I shall roast him about it,* she added mentally. The return to Hollingshead Place could not come soon enough.

Chapter 11
In Which John Pickett's Secret Is Discovered

John Pickett's pace quickened as he crossed the bridge and began the climb to Hollingshead Place. Had he been in London, he would have reported the day's findings to Mr. Colquhoun, but in the absence of the magistrate, Lady Fieldhurst would suffice as confidante and co-conspirator. His heart grew lighter at the thought of the approaching *tête-à-tête.* In some ways, her ladyship's companionship was far superior to that of Mr. Colquhoun.

Upon reaching the house, he entered through the servants' entrance at the rear (thankful to find no sign of the hostile Mrs. Holland) and climbed the back stairs to his attic bedchamber. He opened the door and froze on the threshold. Miss Susannah Hollingshead sat at the head of his narrow cot, reading a small leather-bound volume by the light of a single candle. His stomach lurched as he recognized the book in her hand. Prior to Miss Susannah's invasion, it had resided beneath his mattress.

While he stood motionless in the doorway, she looked up and regarded him steadily.

"You're not really a footman, are you?" It was a statement, not a question.

Pickett, squirming beneath her frank gaze, could not but wonder why, since she was the trespasser, he should be the one to feel guilty.

"I serve Lady Fieldhurst in that capacity, yes," he said, choosing his words with care.

"*Now* you do," she said, acknowledging the literal, if limited, truth of this statement. "But that isn't really who you are, is it? Molly—she's the kitchen maid, do you know her?—says you're not like any footman she's ever seen."

"And why, pray, were you discussing me with Molly?"

Miss Susannah grinned. "Perhaps Miss Grantham was not so very far off the mark when she accused me of gossiping with the servants."

"Apparently you have progressed to plundering their bed-chambers as well."

"Oh, I didn't steal anything! I came to give you this." She held out what appeared to be a large sheet of parchment rolled into a scroll and tied with a yellow ribbon. "But you weren't here, and I remembered that you kept a diary beneath your mattress, and I wondered if—"

She broke off, blushing, and Pickett realized with dismay that Lady Fieldhurst had been right. Miss Susannah, in the throes of a schoolgirl *tendre,* had confiscated his notebook in the hope of discovering some mention of herself. Instead, she had found his notes on the investigation—and now held its success or failure in her hands. Stalling for time while he considered how best to deal with his young admirer, he untied the ribbon and unrolled the parchment. His own face, rendered in charcoal, looked up at him from the curled paper.

"I drew it today, at Mother Shipton's Cave," Miss Susannah offered by way of explanation.

"It's very good."

"I tried to straighten your nose."

"I see that," said Pickett, smiling slightly. "Thank you."

"What—what is it for?" she asked, returning to the subject at hand. "The diary, I mean?"

"What do you think?"

"I think," she said slowly, "that it has something to do with how Mr. Danvers died."

"You are correct. There was reason to suspect the vicarage fire may not have been an accident, so I was sent to find out."

"Sent from where?"

He hesitated only a moment before replying, "London."

"Are you a Bow Street Runner?"

He did not bother to ask how she knew about Bow Street Runners; nothing Miss Susannah Hollingshead said surprised him anymore.

"Yes," he said simply.

"Was he murdered?" she pressed on, wide-eyed.

"I believe so."

"Do you know who did it?"

"No." He was almost glad to be able to answer in the negative; had he admitted to any suspicions, he felt sure Miss Susannah would not rest until he had divulged them.

"What will happen to him when you catch him?" she demanded eagerly. "Will you put his head on a pike on London Bridge?"

He had to smile a little at her confidence that he would apprehend the killer, as well as her assumption that he would personally punish the miscreant for his sins. "Heavens, Miss Susannah, I'm only a keeper of the King's peace. It's not my place to dispense justice." She said nothing, and he felt compelled to add, "Miss Susannah, it's very important that you not tell anyone of this."

"I know," she said solemnly. "I won't tell, I promise."

He did not doubt her sincerity; he only hoped her good intentions would survive her next encounter with a handsome stable hand or an inquisitive chambermaid.

At last, having dispatched the interloper to her own room amid fervent protestations that she would never breathe a word to a living soul, Pickett was free to seek out Lady Fieldhurst. She opened so readily to his faint knock, he could almost flatter himself that she had been awaiting the rendezvous as impatiently as he.

He would have been surprised to know that this fanciful supposition was, in fact, correct. Lady Fieldhurst had found herself impatient for a private interview with her pseudo-servant from the moment she had recognized him in Miss Susannah Hollingshead's *chef d'oeuvre*. Having been first the pampered daughter of a country squire and then the sheltered bride of a domineering man fifteen years her senior, the viscountess was unaccustomed to relating to a man very nearly her own age from a position of equality, let alone superiority. She found such companionship surprisingly agreeable, if occasionally unsettling. Now, however, the sight of Pickett's curling brown hair and plain serge coat forcibly reminded her that he was not really her footman or even her friend, but an instrument of the law. Indeed, there seemed to be little resemblance between the slightly rumpled Bow Street Runner and the powdered and liveried John, except for the nose. And, of course, that mouth . . .

Banishing what threatened to become a highly improper train of thought, she greeted him with polite formality. "Good evening," she said, stepping back from the door to allow him entrance. "I trust you had a pleasant and productive journey."

"It's given me a few things to think about," he acknowledged. "And you?"

"I think you will not be entirely displeased with my efforts."

"I can't imagine anyone being displeased with you, my lady, for any reason," he said warmly.

She smiled, but a shadow crossed her face, and he wondered if she was thinking of her late, unlamented husband. Not for the first time, he thought it rather a pity that someone had been hanged for doing the world in general—and this lady in particular—a favor. But it was not his place to make such observations, so he contented himself with remarking, "I take it you did more than merely explore the beauties of nature."

He had the pleasure, at least, of seeing her abandon her courteous but distant demeanor.

"Pray do not speak to me of the beauties of nature!" she protested, raising her hand to forestall him. "If I never set foot in another cave, it will be all too soon!"

She described, in vivid terms, that moment in the cave when she realized she was lost. Pickett, who had once had a harrowing experience of his own inside a darkened crypt, did not have to feign sympathy for her ladyship's sufferings.

"But I am quite recovered now," the viscountess concluded. "Miss Grantham poured quarts of Mrs. Holland's raspberry cordial down my throat and insisted that I take the bottle up to my room." She indicated a half-empty bottle on the table beside the bed. "Speaking of which, would you care for some refreshment? It is quite good, I must admit."

He shook his head. "Thank you, my lady, but I had best decline."

"Are you certain? It is not very strong, so you need have no fear of overimbibing."

"In truth, my lady, I dare not. If Mrs. Holland should catch a whiff of her prized cordial on my breath, nothing would convince her that I had not been raiding the pantry."

"For shame!" she cried with mock severity. "You deal with thieves and cutthroats on a daily basis, and yet you cry craven at the prospect of facing an angry housekeeper?"

"I can see you've never run afoul of Mrs. Holland."

"Never was I so deceived in anyone! Why, you are nothing but a coward!"

The laughter in her eyes robbed her words of any insult. Lady Fieldhurst could think of at least one instance when he had acted with uncommon bravery and did not hesitate to attribute his professed fear of Mrs. Holland to a rather appealing degree of modesty.

"What can I say?" Pickett wondered aloud, a smile tugging at the corners of his poet's mouth. "My guilty secret is discovered at last."

The light in his brown eyes suggested other secrets waiting to be discovered, and Lady Fieldhurst realized with a start that the room had grown uncomfortably warm. She turned away and busied herself in positioning a screen before the fire. "If we are to speak of guilty secrets, I must tell you that I may have discovered one."

"Indeed?"

"It seems that Mr. Carrington knew Mr. Danvers in India some twenty years ago."

"Did he, now?" Hands clasped loosely behind his back, Pickett paced the floor as he pondered the significance of this revelation.

"According to Mr. Carrington, who had a position there with the East India Company. He said Mr. Danvers was a missionary. I have never seen Will Huggins, but is it possible that he is a half-caste?"

Pickett thought of the young gypsy's black eyes, swarthy skin, and dark, straight hair. "I should think it not only possible, but very probable—although how it might be connected with Mr. Danvers's death escapes me. Did Mr. Carrington make any mention of a scandal linking Danvers with a native woman?"

"Alas, no, although I threw out the most flagrant hints! He gave me nothing beyond a pack of nonsense about the superiority of English ladies compared to their Hindoo counterparts. All very gallant, but ultimately useless."

Thus were Pickett's worst fears realized. At least one gentleman of the party had attempted to flirt with Lady Fieldhurst.

The wholly unreasonable jealousy which assailed him was assuaged slightly by her ladyship's apparent lack of interest in Mr. Carrington except as a source of information.

"It does bring us back to the blackmail theory, though," he said. "If there had been such a scandal, Mr. Carrington would have been in an excellent position to exploit it."

"And just as well, too, for we must acquit Mr. Kendall in that regard. His godmother bequeathed him an independence, so he has sufficient funds for indulging his execrable tastes."

"My lady, you are a marvel! What other information have you contrived to ferret out?"

"Only that we may strike Mr. Meriwether and Miss Hollingshead from the list of possible murderers. It seems they have spent the last few weeks suspecting one another. Oh, and I had the privilege of seeing Miss Susannah Hollingshead's artwork," she added with a mischievous smile. To her surprise, he did not take the bait, but his expression grew solemn.

"Speaking of Miss Susannah, I wasn't lying when I said my guilty secret was discovered. She knows who I am."

"Never say *she* thinks you a coward, too!"

He grinned in spite of himself. "I assure you, I am in deadly earnest. She found the book containing my notes, and realized no footman would keep such a record. I was obliged to confide in her."

"Did you impress upon her the need for secrecy?"

"Yes, and she assures me she will tell no one." He sighed. "I only wish I could believe her."

"I will do her the justice to own that she would not willingly, I think, betray you. Still, it would be a very unusual girl who could keep such a secret at the age of fourteen."

"I feared as much. I'm afraid I will be forced into leaving Yorkshire sooner rather than later." He gave the ghost of a smile. "If Lady Anne should give me the boot, I trust you will be able to make do with her servants."

"Surely you do not think I would stay here if you were sent away?" exclaimed her ladyship, appalled. "No, Mr. Pickett, I would not use you so shabbily, not when you came to Yorkshire at my behest."

"You are very kind, my lady, but there is no need for you to cut short your visit on my account. You can always say that I deceived you, that I gave you falsified references—"

"If you think me capable of such a betrayal, I can only wonder that you answered my summons at all!"

"I would not consider myself betrayed, I assure you. I knew that eventually I must be exposed and that my presence here would no longer be welcome, or even necessary. My only regret is that I have not yet solved the case, nor appear likely to, now. I had hoped that today might bring to light some new revelation, but it does not seem—"

As if on cue, a high-pitched scream shattered the stillness. Pickett and the viscountess exchanged a look of mutual bewilderment, then leaped to their feet as one and ran for the door. The shriek had seemed to come from the floor above, so they hurried down the corridor and pelted up the stairs, joined in their ascent by various other members of the household representing both abovestairs and below.

The third floor, which separated the servants' attic quarters with the family and guest chambers on the level below, comprised the schoolroom and Miss Susannah's bedroom, as well as Miss Grantham's. It was from this latter chamber that the sound had issued, as evidenced by that lady's trembling form drooping against the doorframe and sobbing gustily. Pickett and the viscountess hurried down the uncarpeted corridor to join the little group gathering around her. Thankfully, in the general confusion, no one had noticed that Lady Fieldhurst and Pickett had arrived together and from the general direction of her bedchamber, much less thought to question why this should be so.

"Miss Grantham!" cried Lady Fieldhurst. "What is the—good heavens!"

The governess's rather Spartan little chamber lay in a state of total disarray. The doors of the clothes press stood ajar, and Miss Grantham's meager collection of sober-hued gowns littered the floor around it. The bureau drawers hung open, their contents disgorged. Even the bed had not been left undisturbed: its covers had been thrown back, and the mattress lay upon the bed frame at an awkward angle.

"Here now, what's all this caterwauling?"

Sir Gerald pushed his way through what was by this time a sizeable crowd. Maids and footmen all stepped aside to allow him an uninterrupted view.

"Bless my soul!"

"Pray calm yourself, Miss Grantham," said Lady Anne, gliding past her husband to console the governess. "Yes, it is very shocking, to be sure, but nothing can be gained by these histrionics."

Lady Fieldhurst could only admire her hostess's poise. Lady Anne Hollingshead would never do anything so vulgar as run, and yet she contrived to be on the scene in good time, calmly taking command of the situation. She quickly sent the gawking maids and footmen about their business and instructed her lady's maid to fetch her own smelling salts for Miss Grantham.

"Now," she said when the servants had reluctantly departed, "after you have had a moment to compose yourself, I shall summon a maid to tidy the room. Then we may ascertain whether anything has been taken."

"Oh no, your ladyship," protested Miss Grantham feebly. "I will tidy it myself. I can't bear the thought of the servants' hands on my belongings, not when it might be any one of them who—" She broke off in a fresh bout of tears.

Although Miss Grantham's reservations were unlikely to endear her to the household staff, Lady Fieldhurst could not but feel a certain sympathy for the sentiments that inspired them. Furthermore, on a purely practical level, there was much to be said for restricting access to the room until the culprit could be identified. Unfortunately, the viscountess had no authority to give instructions in a house where she was nothing more than a guest.

"And," concluded Miss Grantham, reemerging from the sodden scrap of linen, "how I shall sleep tonight, when I might be murdered in my bed at any moment, I'm sure I don't know!"

"No one is going to be murdered in bed, on this or any other night," said Lady Anne in a voice which brooked no argument. "Depend upon it, this is nothing more than a mischievous prank—and one for which my daughter will be severely reprimanded."

Lady Fieldhurst felt Pickett stiffen, and when she glanced up at him, it was to find him frowning thoughtfully into space.

"If I may make a suggestion," she said, "perhaps it would be best if Miss Grantham slept elsewhere tonight. I should be happy to trade places—"

"Pray do not encourage her in these flights of fancy," protested Lady Anne. "There is not the slightest need for you to give up your room. If Miss Grantham is unwilling to remain in her own room, I shall have a truckle bed set up in Miss Susannah's room. If they are a bit crowded as a result, perhaps it will serve as a lesson to them both," she added severely in an aside clearly meant for the governess.

"Thank you, my lady," Miss Grantham said meekly. "I would be most grateful, although I should hesitate to leave my belongings unprotected." She glanced around the untidy room as if the value of its meager contents rivaled that of the crown jewels.

"Quite understandable, Miss Grantham," Lady Fieldhurst said hastily. "May I suggest that my own John stand guard tonight? His innocence in the matter is unquestionable, for he has only just returned from an errand in Knaresborough, and would have had no opportunity to ransack your room."

So dazzled was Pickett by the sound of her ladyship's voice claiming him as her own that, of its own volition, his face assumed that blank expression deemed suitable for servants. Miss Grantham gave him a long, measuring look and, apparently pleased with what she saw in spite of his lack of powder and livery, nodded her approval.

Chapter 12

In Which John Pickett Reads a Dull Book, and Makes an Interesting Discovery

"Well?" prompted Lady Fieldhurst, after the crisis was past and the governess was securely installed in Miss Susannah's bedroom. "Aren't you going to thank me?"

"Thank you?" echoed Pickett. "Thank you for volunteering me to stand guard all night over Miss Grantham's room?"

"What rot!" retorted her ladyship inelegantly. "Admit it! You have been champing at the bit to search this room for yourself ever since you discovered that it had been ransacked. I merely gave you a convenient opportunity to do so. I take it you disagree with Lady Anne's conviction that it was merely Miss Susannah in a mischievous mood?"

"Yes, I do. Miss Susannah, you will remember, was in my room."

"But who would have reason to do such a thing? And what possible connection can Miss Grantham's room have with Mr. Danvers's death? As far as I can tell, the only connection between her and Mr. Danvers is a case of unrequited love on her part, and a ponderously long—" She broke off, her eyes widening in dawning comprehension. "John!"

"Exactly. We come back to the manuscript."

"Something must be hidden in it," conceded her ladyship. "But what could be so important that someone would risk such an act of vandalism in a house full of people?"

"When we find the 'what,' I think we'll have the 'who,' " Pickett said. "And as for the house being full of people—I wonder if it was."

"You think the damage may have been done before the pleasure party had returned? But surely Miss Grantham must have noticed it before now!"

"Not if she had been kept busy elsewhere—in the schoolroom, perhaps. Unfortunately, in my present guise I can hardly ask her for an accounting of her movements."

"Perhaps *you* cannot, but *I* can," declared Lady Fieldhurst, striding across the room to the wardrobe. "There must be something in here which a thoughtful guest might consider indispensable to Miss Grantham's comfort. A book perhaps?" She examined a motley collection of worn-looking volumes. "Perhaps poetry to soothe the nerves? Oh, look! *The Castle of Otranto!* Well! It is just as I always suspected: our Miss Grantham is a *devotée* of gothic romances. But she will not want Miss Susannah to see her reading such a thrilling tale. I think—yes, Hannah More should do the trick. Her works are so very improving, not only would Lady Anne find them unobjectionable, but they are guaranteed to put even the most troubled mind to sleep."

Having decided the matter, she pulled the book from its resting place and sailed from the room. She returned a short time later without the book and with a mixed report.

"I have good news and bad," she said with a sigh. "As you supposed, upon returning from our outing, Miss Grantham went straight to the schoolroom. She did not go to her room until quite recently, when she discovered it in its disheveled state."

"Then the room may well have been ransacked while most of the family was absent. No doubt the culprit was searching for the manuscript, not realizing Miss Grantham had taken it with her."

"Yes, well, that brings us to the bad news. Miss Grantham

still has it with her and refuses to let it out of her sight."

"Then she knows it was the target of the search."

"Perhaps," her ladyship said thoughtfully, "but I don't think so. I think her attachment to it is mostly a sentimental one. I fear I have done Miss Susannah a grave disservice. I suggested to Miss Grantham that, if Miss Susannah had indeed wrecked her room as a prank, she might inflict similar damage on the manuscript while her governess slept. I left Miss Grantham with the expressed intention of reading aloud to her charge selections from Miss More's works in the hope that they may improve her character. I only hope that someday Miss Susannah may find it in her heart to forgive me!"

It soon appeared that Lady Fieldhurst had done her work well. Shortly after the viscountess had returned to her own chamber and the house settled down to slumber, Pickett's search of the wardrobe was interrupted by the rattle of the doorknob. He started guiltily and scarcely had time to stuff a very dull collection of letters back into the bureau drawer before the door opened to admit Miss Grantham clutching a thick sheaf of papers to her bony chest.

"I suppose I had best leave this with you for safekeeping," she said, thrusting her burden into his arms before turning and leaving the room without another word.

Alone once more, Pickett looked down at the stack of papers in his arms. Somewhere within these sheets, he was convinced, lay the key to a murder. He locked the door, then sat down on the bed and leafed through page after page of closely written script. At last, having reached the end, he sighed gustily. Whatever else it might contain, the manuscript concealed no cryptic messages or clandestine correspondence. Perhaps he had been wrong after all, and the vicar's book was nothing more than a ponderous history which no one—aside from its author, at any rate—would care to read.

There was only one way to find out, and, since he had no doubt Miss Grantham would require the return of the manuscript the following morning, he was unlikely to have another chance. Steeling himself for the tedious task which awaited him, he stripped off his coat, waistcoat, and cravat, then stretched out on the bed, propping himself on his elbow, and began to read.

According to the Domesday Book of 1086, the plot of Land we know today as the Village of Kendall was originally part of a much larger Tract granted to one Gerald de Holineside by William I in 1067 as a reward for Military Services rendered during said William's conquest of these Fair Shores . . .

By the time Pickett had waded through fifty pages of the vicar's stilted prose, his eyes were beginning to glaze over. When a soft knock on the door interrupted his reading, he felt no sense of guilt or urgency, nothing but relief at being granted an unexpected reprieve. However, he was not so forgetful of the need for secrecy as to leave the manuscript lying on the bed in plain sight. He pushed the stack of pages beneath the bed, then unlocked the door to admit his nocturnal visitor. To his surprise and delight, the woman on the other side was not Miss Grantham. Instead, the viscountess stood there clad in a ruffled pink dressing gown, her blond hair tied loosely back at the nape of her neck. Pickett, his brain still fuzzy from the vicar's tome, wondered with detached interest whether he had in fact fallen asleep over the manuscript, and was now dreaming. If so, he was in no hurry to awaken.

"My lady! You should not be up at this hour," he protested, stepping aside to allow her entrance nonetheless.

"Nor should you, for that matter," she replied. "I thought if you had found anything of interest by now, you surely must have come to tell me. Since you had not, I feared you must be in for rather a long night of it and thought you might be glad of some refreshment."

He noticed for the first time that she had not come empty handed. She carried a black bottle and a long-stemmed glass, both of which she set on Miss Grantham's small, scarred writing table.

"The ubiquitous raspberry cordial," she explained. "I fear I have only the one glass. I have been drinking from it, but I dared not send down to the kitchen for another. Or would you prefer to drink from the bottle?"

Pickett, having not the slightest objection to placing his lips where her ladyship's had once been, assured her that it did not matter.

Lady Fieldhurst dispensed the sweet red cordial into the glass and handed it to him. "Am I correct, then, in assuming that you found no secret messages hidden between the sheets—er, pages?" inquired her ladyship, her gaze shying away from the rumpled, narrow bed.

"You are."

He took the glass from her hand and drank greedily from it. As the viscountess had said, it was quite good, and at another time he might have smiled at the notion of giving Mrs. Holland his compliments. Tonight, however, he had other, more important matters on his mind.

"What will you do now?" asked the viscountess.

"I'm afraid there's nothing for it but to read the thing all the way through."

Lady Fieldhurst was appalled. "In *one night?*"

"I'm unlikely to get another chance."

"Very well." She settled herself on the uncomfortable straight chair before the writing table. "You can read half, and I shall take the other half. You have only to tell me what to look for."

Pickett smiled. "You're very good, my lady, but there lies the trouble. I don't know myself what to look for—if there is anything at all, which I am beginning to doubt."

"It sounds terribly tedious."

"It is."

"Shall I bear you company, then?" Reading rejection in his eyes, she hurried into speech before he could voice it. "I know you will say that it would be highly improper for me to do so, but surely we have already spent so much time together *tête-à-tête* that such considerations need hardly weigh with us at this late date."

She colored a little at the recollection that none of their previous assignations had been conducted in a bedchamber, with both of them in various stages of undress. The memory of that kiss in the library hung in the air between them. Still, she made no attempt to withdraw the offer, and Pickett was sorely tempted to accept it. Alas, Duty, that harshest of taskmasters, prevailed.

"I am truly grateful for the offer, my lady, but if I'm to go chasing after mares' nests, I think it best that I keep a clear head."

"Why, John!" She rose from her chair smiled up at him, one eyebrow ironically arched. "I think that is quite the prettiest compliment I have ever received."

Then, having reduced him to stammering incoherence, she exited the room, shutting the door softly behind her.

Pickett, alone once again and more reluctant than ever to spend what little remained of the night reading the vicar's history, nevertheless stretched out on the bed and picked up the manuscript where he had left off.

Although the book was primarily a history of the parish and its church, there were numerous references to milestones in the life of the principal families. Sprinkled amongst the construction of the bell tower and the casting of its four enormous bells were accounts of the crusading Holineside who never reached Jerusalem, having succumbed to dysentery before ever crossing the Channel; the seventeenth-century baronet, now known as Hollinside, who contrived to lie low during the Civil War and consequently kept his holdings intact; and, not coincidentally, the rise of the rival Kendall family, who took a bolder stand against Cromwell and were rewarded after the Restoration with a barony. Pickett's eyes burned and his candle slowly melted down to a misshapen lump of wax, but still he plowed on. It was not until he had turned the three hundredth page and entered the eighteenth century (by which time the church had acquired a new organ, and the village had been moved to a new location some distance from the river) that something in the text caught his attention. He sat up, drawing the candle nearer, and read the entry again, taking particular notice of the date: 21 October 1704. He thumbed ahead three pages—no, five—to the events of the following summer, then turned back to re-read the earlier entry.

This was it, then, the secret he had been hoping to find. For this, one man had been killed, and countless others robbed. He glanced at the tiny window, where the black night was already beginning to give way to gray dawn. He must get what rest he could, for it promised to be a very busy day. He snuffed out the candle, collapsed against the pillow, and slept.

When Pickett next opened his eyes, the sun was high in the sky. He leaped up with a guilty start and reached for the coat and waistcoat he had tossed aside several hours earlier. At any moment Miss Grantham might reappear, demanding the safe return of her property. Surely, he thought, she was not so familiar with the manuscript's bulk that she would notice the temporary absence of a few crucial passages. He removed the pertinent pages, folded them, and tucked them into the inside pocket of his coat. A short time later, he assured a grateful Miss Grantham that no intruders had disturbed the sanctity of her bedchamber during the night, then climbed the narrow, uncarpeted stairs to his own attic room. He reached beneath the mattress and removed the notebook and the hollow wooden tipstaff which served as his badge of office. Correctly assuming that the family would still be abed, he eschewed the servants' stairs leading down to the kitchen and took the main staircase instead. Mrs. Holland, he knew, would have much to say about such presumption, but he had no time for her inevitable tirade; as of today, his career as a footman was over.

He paused when he reached the floor where Lady Fieldhurst's bedchamber was located. Her ladyship would expect to be informed of his discovery. One might even argue that he owed her an explanation, since it was her summons that had first brought him to Yorkshire. Still, he thought it best to leave her curiosity unsatisfied, at least for the nonce. She had already had one encounter with a killer, which had almost turned deadly when the killer realized the fatal secret was out; better to risk her ladyship's displeasure than to place her in harm's way. He continued down the stairs to the ground floor, let himself out the massive front doors, and set out in the direction of the Kendall estate.

He stopped first at the church and, after some stumbling about in the semidarkness of the nave, finally found what he sought on a shelf built into the lectern. He breathed a sigh of relief, for without this final piece of the puzzle, all his other efforts would have been useless. He slipped his prize into his coat pocket along with the manuscript pages, then resumed his errand.

The sunshine of the last several days had given way to heavy gray clouds, and the frequent gusts of wind smelled like rain. As Pickett entered the village, he saw shopkeepers and housewives hurrying about their chores, trying to complete their outside tasks before the weather drove them indoors. It seemed somehow surprising that life for others should go on just as it had before, unmindful of the fact that one of their neighbors would soon hang for what they believed to be no more than a tragic accident. Of course, Londoners were often equally oblivious to the dealings of their fellow men, but Pickett had always supposed that country people kept few secrets from one another. In this case, at least, he could not have been more mistaken; what these people did not know about one of their most prominent families could fill a book—and had.

On the other side of the village, he turned at a scrolled wrought-iron gate and trudged up a tree-lined drive to the elegant redbrick edifice that was the Kendall residence, then rapped on the massive oak door with the end of his tipstaff.

"I'm sorry, sir, but his lordship is at breakfast," said the footman who answered the door, when Pickett requested an audience with Lord Kendall.

"You may offer him my apologies for interrupting him," said Pickett, opening his hand to reveal a silver shilling lying in the palm of his hand. Seeing the man was still unconvinced, he added, "I would not ask if it were not important."

The footman struggled with himself, looked longingly at the coin in Pickett's hand, and came to a decision. Snatching the coin away as if fearful Pickett would change his mind, he pocketed it and sketched a stiff bow.

"If you would care to wait in the study, sir, I'll fetch his lordship."

He led the way to a small, dark room dominated by a cluttered desk at one end, indicated that Pickett might seat himself on the single straight chair backed up against the wall, and went in search of his lordship.

It soon became evident that Lord Kendall was one of those

persons who did not appear at his best until sufficient quantities of coffee had been pumped into his system. Stalking into the study with the air of a bear awakened early from hibernation, he looked Pickett up and down for a long moment, then demanded, "Well? Am I supposed to know you?"

Fortunately, Pickett was too accustomed to Mr. Colquhoun's surlier moods to be intimidated. "We have never met, my lord, although you may have seen me recently at Hollingshead Place," he replied, bowing. "I have been acting as footman to Lady Fieldhurst."

" 'Acting as'?" echoed Lord Kendall, suspicion now added to belligerence. "A curious choice of words, sir. Am I to understand, then, that you are, in fact, *not* Lady Fieldhurst's footman?"

In spite of Lord Kendall's apparent hostility, Pickett could not but be grateful for the man's quick wits. That, at least, should speed matters along. "Your understanding is correct, my lord. Allow me to introduce myself: John Pickett, Bow Street police office."

Lord Kendall's scowl abated somewhat. "Then I gather this is not a social call. How may I be of service to you?"

"I have been reliably informed that you are the local Justice of the Peace. I should like you, in that capacity, to issue an arrest warrant."

"Very well," said Lord Kendall, seating his bulk behind the desk and pulling open one of its drawers. "For whom, pray?"

Pickett told him.

"Bless my soul!" blustered his lordship. "On what charge?"

"The murder of Cyril Danvers will do, for a start."

"I trust you have sufficient evidence for such a claim?"

Pickett stiffened. "I assure you, I would not send a human being to the gallows on anything less."

He produced the purloined manuscript pages from his coat

pocket. "I understand you dined with the Hollingsheads on the evening of the murder, so I need not tell you what happened that night. I think this may explain the rest."

He surrendered the papers to Lord Kendall and waited in expectant silence while his lordship retrieved a pair of wire-rimmed spectacles from his waistcoat pocket, affixed them to the bridge of his nose, and examined the pages.

"An interesting theory, I'll admit, though hardly a new one in these parts," pronounced the Justice of the Peace at last. "Have you any proof?"

"I have." Pickett produced a yellowed sheet of foolscap whose ragged edge testified to its having been torn from a bound volume. Lord Kendall studied the words painstakingly transcribed thereupon.

"Very well," he said at last, shaking his grizzled head. "God knows it's an ugly job, but I know my duty."

For the next several moments there was no sound in the study but the scratching of pen on parchment. His duty done, Lord Kendall shook sand over the document to absorb the wet ink, then rolled it up and handed it to Pickett.

"Thank you, my lord," said Pickett, storing it inside his hollow tipstaff. "May I leave this with you for safekeeping?" He gestured toward the torn paper still lying on the desk.

"Yes, of course. I'll see to it until it can be restored to its rightful place. Shall I come with you?" offered his lordship. "Help out, in case it's needed?"

"Thank you, my lord," said Pickett again, "but I'm sure I can manage."

"Are you quite certain? You look rather young for this line of work."

There it was again, the inevitable reference to his age, or lack thereof. "I've been with Bow Street these last five years, sir."

While this assertion was true, in the strictest sense, Pickett saw no need to mention the fact that he had been a Runner for less than a twelvemonth. Lord Kendall was evidently satisfied, for he gave a nod, shook hands with Pickett, and returned to his interrupted breakfast.

Tipstaff in hand, Pickett trudged back through the village and down the slope to the bridge spanning the river. Although he could not deny a certain satisfaction at having solved a perplexing puzzle, he took no joy in the task which lay ahead. Arresting a killer was nothing new, but doing so after having shared the same roof with the murderer for almost a fortnight was quite another matter.

He crossed the temporary wooden bridge and followed the road up the hill and around a curve. A movement off in the distance caught his eye, and he saw Sir Gerald Hollingshead standing on the riverbank struggling with his fishing line, which appeared to have snagged in the branches of a low-hanging willow. Leaving the road bed, Pickett set out across the grass in the baronet's direction.

"What, ho? Damned thing's caught in a tree," exclaimed Sir Gerald with unimpaired good humor. "Oh, it's you—John, is it? You'd best get back to the house. Your mistress wasn't best pleased with your absence at breakfast."

"I daresay her ladyship will contrive to rub along well enough without me," Pickett said with a wistful smile. "Sir Gerald, I have a confession to make. I'm afraid Lady Fieldhurst and I have enjoyed your hospitality under false pretenses. I came at her ladyship's summons, but I am not her footman. In fact—"

"Oh, I know all about that." Sir Gerald chuckled. "Gave my Emma a rare turn, stumbling across you and her ladyship like that, but her mama explained to her that such goings-on aren't uncommon for a widow-woman as young as her ladyship, so there's no harm done. Least said, soonest mended, I always say."

"Yes, sir, but you don't understand. My name is John Pickett. I represent the Bow Street police office."

Sir Gerald dropped his fishing rod, leaving it dangling from the willow branches, and planted his hands on his hips. "What the—? I think you had best explain yourself, sirrah!"

"I think you know the rest," Pickett continued, unruffled. "I was summoned here to investigate the murder of Mr. Cyril Danvers."

Sir Gerald's face turned ashen. "Murder? Nonsense! Danvers died accidentally, when the vicarage was struck by lightning. Everyone knows that!"

"That is certainly what everyone was meant to believe. But I examined the body before it was buried. Mr. Danvers died of a blow to his head from a heavy object—most probably the poker I found lying on the floor of the burned-out shell."

Sir Gerald opened his mouth as if to protest, but no sound emerged.

"Sir Gerald Hollingshead," Pickett continued, "in the name of His Majesty, King George the Third, I arrest you for the murder of Cyril Danvers."

In his brief Bow Street career, Pickett had been cursed, kicked, sucker punched, and spat upon by those felons he was called upon to bring to justice. Sir Gerald did none of these things. In fact, his shoulders slumped forward as if grateful to be relieved of a burden too heavy to bear. When at last he spoke again, Pickett had the impression he was repeating an argument he had made many times to himself over the last few weeks.

"He didn't suffer. He never felt a thing. I'm strong as a man half my age," Sir Gerald said with simple pride. "One blow was all it took. He never felt a thing."

"At first," Pickett said slowly, "I thought the vicarage must have been set afire to destroy any evidence of murder. But that wasn't the real reason, was it?"

"That damned book!" groaned Sir Gerald, the color returning to his face in a rush of crimson. "That bloody boring book that no one in his right mind would ever want to read! I thought I had destroyed it—and then to find out that it was under my own roof all along!"

"It was you, then, who ransacked Miss Grantham's room?"

"Aye, I might as well be hanged for a sheep as for a lamb. Not that it did me any good, for I never did find the thing—although *you* appeared to have no trouble in doing so," he added resentfully.

"Miss Grantham gave it to me for safekeeping," Pickett explained. "Tell me, Sir Gerald, how long have you known? That you were not the true baronet, I mean?"

Sir Gerald heaved a sigh. "Not until the night of that accursed dinner. Oh, there had been talk amongst the village folk years ago, when the old woman died, but no one pays any heed to that sort of thing."

"And on the night of the dinner party?"

"Old Danvers was blathering on about his book, as usual, and interrupted himself to tell me he wished to speak to me about a matter of some importance. I assumed he wanted a donation for repairing the roof, or restoring the bell tower, or some such thing. I brought him to my study after dinner and started to write him out a bank draft, but he turned it down, spouting a lot of nonsense about how he knew I would want to do the right thing by Mr. Meriwether. When I realized what was in the wind, well, I knew what I had to do. The bridge had washed out, and in all the confusion, I walked down to the vicarage. You know the rest."

"It must have seemed intolerable, the idea of losing everything to your daughter's rejected suitor," Pickett observed.

"Harder for my wife, I think, than for me. I've nothing against young Meriwether, seems to me a steady sort of fellow, but my wife wants something better for Emma. That's why I did it, you know. For Anne."

"Oh?" Whatever justification Pickett might have expected Sir Gerald to offer for his crime, this was not it.

"She was the daughter of the Earl of Claridge. When I first met her, she was only seventeen years old, and had just become betrothed. Her fiancé was a captain of the Hussars and the heir to a marquisate." Sir Gerald's eyes glazed over as if reliving that long-ago meeting. "Not that it would have done me any good even if she'd been free. She was beautiful, elegant, and cultured, and I—well, I was little more than a middle-aged country squire come to the Metropolis for the first time. Why would she think of me when she could have a dashing young cavalryman in scarlet and gold lace?"

"And yet she married you, not him," Pickett pointed out.

"Aye, she did," acknowledged Sir Gerald, obviously taking no pleasure in the fact. "Her handsome young Hussar was killed at Gibraltar, and it soon appeared that the two of them had anticipated the marriage vows. Her family needed a husband for her in a hurry, and I was too flattered to wonder at their sudden encouragement of my suit."

Pickett, struggling to reconcile the haughty Lady Anne Hollingshead with the eager young lover Sir Gerald described, was suddenly struck by the implications of this confession. "Then—Miss Hollingshead—?"

"No, no, Emma is mine, and so are Philip and Sukey. Anne miscarried. The midwife said it would have been a boy." Sir Gerald shook his head wonderingly. "God help me, my first thought was relief that Hollingshead Place wouldn't go to another man's child. We've never spoken of the babe from that day to this, but I can't go past the churchyard without seeing how carefully his grave is tended. No, she still loves her fallen soldier. Daresay she always will."

"But you stood by her when another man might have cast her off," said Pickett, finding himself in the curious position of having to comfort a killer. "She must have been grateful."

"Aye, that's what I had hoped for," Sir Gerald confessed with a heavy sigh. "I told myself that love had been known to grow from shakier beginnings, but I reckoned without the Claridge pride. Anne thought I'd allowed myself to be tricked into matrimony, and she could never feel anything but mild contempt for a fellow she considered a dupe."

"I'm sorry," said Pickett, and was surprised to find that he meant it.

"The baronetcy was the only thing that made me even remotely acceptable to her as a suitor," Sir Gerald continued. "The idea of losing it—well, it was more than I could bear. Tell me, Mr. Pickett, have you a wife?"

Pickett blinked at the sudden *non sequitur.* "No, sir."

"I thought not. Take a word of advice from one older and wiser: never woo where you cannot hope to win. That way lies madness."

Pickett thought of a certain midnight embrace in Sir Gerald's own library and nodded. "I'll remember it, sir."

"Now," said Sir Gerald, withdrawing a knife from his coat pocket and cutting the recalcitrant fishing line, "I daresay you and Kendall have a great deal of work to do, so we'd best be on our way." He saw Pickett eyeing the blade warily, and returned it to his pocket. "Never fear, I'll go quietly."

He stepped back from the bank and turned in a slow half circle, lovingly surveying for the last time the slope of the fertile fields, the gray stone house crowning the hill, and the lush wood beyond.

"Philip never loved the land the way I did. I rode the boy

hard about it—too hard, maybe—but perhaps it's all for the best. I only wish there was some way to spare Anne and the girls."

Pickett could think of one such way, but he hesitated to mention it. He was a Bow Street Runner, an instrument of the King's justice. He was not at all sure he had the right—never mind the authority—to grant a condemned man's last wish. There was no excuse, no possible justification for Sir Gerald's actions, and yet he could not help feeling pity for this man who had loved so devotedly, and received so little in return.

Still, the question remained: what constituted justice where murder was concerned? At the end of the day, the victim would still be dead, and no trial by jury would ever bring him back. Surely Mr. Danvers was beyond caring whether his killer's execution was public or private. Sir Gerald had already lost everything that had given his life meaning; any further punishment seemed superfluous.

"The river is still high, and the current is strong," Pickett said at last. "Any man unfortunate enough to fall in would most likely drown before he reached the bridge."

Sir Gerald gave him a long, steady look. "I daresay you're right."

Pickett turned and began walking up the slope away from the river. He heard a splash and turned back. There was no sign of Sir Gerald at all, only his fishing rod still hanging from the tree and the swift, silent waters rushing downstream toward the bridge.

Chapter 13

In Which the Truth Is Revealed

Lady Fieldhurst, having spent an interminable breakfast waiting in vain for Pickett to appear, retired to the drawing room with the Hollingshead ladies, where she spent the better part of the morning making desultory conversation with Lady Anne and Miss Hollingshead, playing halfhearted duets with Miss Susannah upon the pianoforte, and assisting Philip in the construction of a house of cards. The promise of inclement weather made outdoor activity unwise, although this had not deterred Sir Gerald from setting out with his fishing rod immediately after breakfast. It seemed to Lady Fieldhurst as if the entire household were in a state of suspended animation, waiting for something, only God—or perhaps John Pickett—knew what.

The brooding atmosphere was lightened somewhat by the arrival of Mr. Jasper Carrington, come to reiterate his pleasure in the previous day's outing, and to express his gratitude at having been invited to participate. Mr. Colin Meriwether soon arrived, ostensibly on the same errand, although anyone observing Miss Hollingshead's glowing countenance as his name was announced would have little difficulty in discerning the true reason for his visit. Mr. Robert Kendall's arrival some moments later came as no surprise, although Lady Fieldhurst was somewhat taken aback to discover that his parents had accompanied him. With the exception of Sir Gerald—and, of course, Mr. Danvers—the party was exactly as it had been on the night of Mr. Danvers's death.

Apparently Lady Anne also sensed that the party was now complete, for it was at this juncture that she instructed the butler to bring tea and cakes. He had no sooner departed on this errand than the massive front door opened one more time, and Lady Fieldhurst heard the butler address the newcomer in tones no servant would dream of assuming toward a guest.

"So *there* you are, and high time, too! First absent at breakfast, and now here you are out of livery, strolling in the front door as if you were one of the family! I hope you have an adequate excuse for your conduct?"

"I do," the newcomer replied curtly, and Lady Fieldhurst's pulse quickened at the sound of the voice she had been listening for all morning.

A moment later he strode into the drawing room, not John the footman, but John Pickett the Bow Street Runner, wearing a coat of brown serge and sober yet determined expression.

"John!" cried the viscountess in some distress, quite forgetting that she was supposed to be his irate employer. "Where have you been? When you did not appear at breakfast, I imagined the most dreadful possibilities!"

He silenced her with one brief but speaking look before addressing himself to Lady Anne.

"I'm afraid I have bad news, my lady," he said, removing his shallow-crowned hat as he approached the baronet's widow. "Sir Gerald has fallen into the river and drowned." While she digested this pronouncement, Pickett turned to the butler. "The current is so strong that he'll be washed downstream if we don't step lively. Send a contingent of footmen and stable hands down to the river to recover the body."

The Hollingshead butler, having been in service to the family for most of his fifty-odd years, was not in the habit of taking orders from a mere footman, particularly one young enough to be his son, but he nevertheless responded to the ring of authority in Pickett's voice.

"Y-yes, sir," he said, backing away toward the door. "I will attend to it at once."

Throughout this exchange, Lady Anne remained seated with rigidly correct posture upon a striped satin chair, looking as if she had been turned to marble. No emotion showed in her handsome countenance, and Lady Fieldhurst found herself thinking of those objects left within the petrifying well. Miss Hollingshead, by contrast, had turned alarmingly pale, and Mr. Meriwether moved quickly to stand beside her, taking her trembling hand in his. Miss Susannah, face flushed crimson, leaped up from the pianoforte and confronted Pickett.

"*You* did this!" she cried. "It's all your fault, and I *hate* you!"

Pickett flinched as if she had struck him. For the first time, Lady Fieldhurst wondered if the girl's *tendre* was as unrequited as she had supposed. There were, after all, only ten years between her fourteen and his four-and-twenty—significantly less than the fifteen-year difference which had separated the viscountess from her late husband. She was possessed of a sudden urge to box Miss Susannah's ears.

In this desire, at least, she was not alone. "If you cannot control yourself, Susannah, you may return to the schoolroom," Lady Anne addressed her younger daughter in frigid tones.

"Pray don't scold her, your ladyship," protested Pickett, pale but resolute. "She is closer to the truth than you know. I am not a footman at all, but John Pickett of the Bow Street police office. At the time of Sir Gerald's, er, unfortunate accident, I was in the process of placing him under arrest for the murder of Cyril Danvers."

Lady Anne regarded him with stern disapproval. "If this is intended to be a joke, young man, I confess I fail to see the humor in it."

Pickett uncapped his tipstaff and produced the rolled-up

paper bearing Lord Kendall's signature. "I assure you, your ladyship, I would not joke about such a thing."

"And why, pray, would my husband murder the vicar?"

"Because of his book."

Lady Anne raised a skeptical eyebrow. "I will be the first to concede that my husband is—was—hardly a patron of the arts, but to suggest that he would kill a man for writing a tedious book is preposterous."

"I'm afraid that the book wasn't nearly tedious enough for Sir Gerald, ma'am. While researching the church records, Mr. Danvers found evidence of a marriage early in the last century, between a village girl and the eldest son of the second baronet."

"Yes, but the marriage was a sham," put in Mr. Meriwether. "He wanted only to seduce the poor girl and could not persuade her any other way."

"So the Hollingshead family has always insisted, and their word has always been accepted in the village as law," Pickett said. "In fact, the marriage was plainly recorded in the church register, but the page was torn out and concealed within the spine. Apparently the priest who performed the ceremony feared reprisals from his patron. Perhaps he would have come forward with proof after the birth of the child; we'll never know for certain. At any rate, the vicar died only weeks after the wedding, and the new incumbent was apparently content to let his curate deal with the day-to-day business of the parish, and so he never bothered to read through his predecessor's papers. By the time the child, a boy, was born the following summer, his father had been killed in a tavern brawl on the Continent, and so the heir to the baronetcy was raised as a bastard."

"Sir! I must ask you to watch your language!" protested Miss Grantham, clapping her hands over Miss Susannah's ears.

"I beg your pardon, Miss Grantham," Pickett said meekly. "To continue, on the night of the dinner party, Mr. Danvers informed Sir Gerald of his findings, assuming that he would want to do the noble thing and set the record straight. He could not have been more mistaken. After the party broke up and it was discovered that the bridge had washed out, Sir Gerald took advantage of the confusion to walk to the vicarage. Perhaps he tried to persuade Mr. Danvers to strike that passage from his manuscript; perhaps he even tried to buy his silence. Whatever the case, his efforts were unsuccessful, so he picked up the poker from the fireplace and struck Mr. Danvers in the head with it."

"But I thought he shot him," protested Lady Fieldhurst. "In fact, I heard the gunshot myself."

Pickett smiled at her. "An honest mistake, my lady. In fact, I had to trip over the murder weapon—literally—before I tumbled to the truth. Even with Mr. Danvers dead, Sir Gerald still had to destroy the book, lest someone else should read it and reach the same conclusions as the vicar. When he couldn't find it after a brief but no doubt frantic search, he set the room on fire. You may remember that Mr. Danvers had been having trouble with gypsies stealing his chickens and had purchased a fowling piece. The gun was mounted over the mantel, along with a horn of powder. The 'gunshot' you heard was undoubtedly the flames setting off the powder."

Pickett fell silent, and Emma Hollingshead spoke into the void. "But—but if the marriage was binding, and Papa was not the true baronet, then that—then that means—" She broke off, staring up at Mr. Meriwether.

"Quite right, Miss Hollingshead." Pickett turned to the curate, who still held tightly to his beloved's hand. "No doubt there will be a few legal hoops to jump through first, but you had best get used to hearing yourself addressed as Sir Colin Hollingshead."

"At a cost of two men's lives," said the new baronet, shaking his head in bewildered disbelief. "I would not have wanted it at such a price."

"Harrumph!" Lord Kendall cleared his throat. "No sense in feeling guilty over something that's none of your doing, my boy."

Mr. Carrington seconded this sentiment. "Through his death, Mr. Danvers set to right an ancient wrong. I think he would be pleased."

"I fear you have allowed tavern gossip to cloud your judgment, Mr. Pickett," said Lady Anne. "Have you any proof of this extraordinary claim?"

"Indeed, I have, your ladyship. Only this morning I stopped at the church and found the page torn from the church register pushed down behind the spine, just as Mr. Danvers wrote in his book."

Philip Hollingshead, who had had nothing to say thus far to the destruction of his birthright, suddenly leaped to his feet and ran from the room. In seconds he could be seen from the windows, running down the path leading to the church.

"I say!" exclaimed Mr. Carrington, leaping up as if to set out in pursuit.

Pickett shook his head. "Let him go. He can't do any harm."

Mr. Carrington wrestled with indecision. "But—the evidence—"

"I left it with Lord Kendall for safekeeping," said Pickett, bowing slightly in his direction. "You still have it, sir?"

The Justice of the Peace nodded. "Locked up pending the trial. Unnecessary, as it turns out, but at least that young hothead will never get at it. Pity the boy has to lose his inheritance, though."

Mr. Carrington begged leave to differ. "I confess, I don't know the lad well, but I knew many such young men in the East. I suspect that eventually he might be happier as a soldier or a sailor than he ever would have as a country landowner."

Miss Susannah looked up, puffy-eyed, as realization of this fresh loss dawned on her. "But—but if everything belongs to Cousin Colin now, what will happen to the rest of us?"

"There will always be a place for you here, Susannah," Mr. Meriwether assured her. "You have my word on it."

Lady Anne, at least, was unmoved by this display of generosity. "Your sense of duty is admirable, Cousin, but I will not be a pensioner in the same house where I was once mistress. Every feeling revolts! No, my children and I will remove to Claridge Hall. I believe the Dower House is vacant; I am sure my brother, the earl, will not object to our occupying it."

"Perhaps *he* may not, but *I* shall," Emma Hollingshead spoke up with uncharacteristic firmness. "You may reside wherever you please, Mama, but I intend to remain here and marry Colin. There can be no question of a London Season now, so long as we are in mourning, and even *you* cannot suppose there would be many eligible gentlemen eager to wed the daughter of a discredited baronet."

To Lady Fieldhurst's surprise, Lady Anne accepted her daughter's show of independence with every appearance of resignation. "You are right, alas. And when I think of the brilliant match you might have achieved! Ah well, I suppose there is no use in pining for what might have been." She rose from her chair with great dignity, and addressed the company, "And now, if you will excuse me, I must change my gown for something more sober, as befits my newly widowed status. I suggest, Emma, that you do the same. Miss Grantham, the gray muslin will suffice for Miss Susannah until some of her dresses may be dyed."

Miss Grantham rose obediently and began to herd her charge toward the door. As she drew abreast of Pickett, he detained her.

"One moment, Miss Grantham. I have something which belongs to you." He reached into the inside pocket of his coat, and drew out the folded pages of manuscript. "I hope you will forgive me for borrowing them. I assure you, I took very good care of them."

The governess blinked at the papers as if seeing them for the first time. "Oh, dear! What will happen to Mr. Danvers's book now?"

"Perhaps that decision should be left to his son," suggested Pickett.

"Mr. Danvers had no son," Miss Grantham reminded him. "The poor man never married."

"It is true that he never married," Pickett conceded, "but it appears that while he was in India he, er, formed an illicit union with a native woman and fathered a son by her. He brought the infant back to England with him, and placed him with a couple whose own child had just died. The boy lived with them until their deaths. Since then, ironically enough, he's lived almost on the vicarage doorstep—one of the gypsies Mr. Danvers was so determined to—"

A loud crash interrupted Pickett's conclusion. Mr. Carrington, ashen faced, had dropped his teacup, and a puddle of the dark liquid now spread across the floor at his feet. "What—what did you say?"

"Mr. Danvers had an illegitimate son while in India. He brought the child to England, and the boy—almost a man now—has been living amongst the gypsies in the Home Wood."

Mr. Carrington shook his head. "No. Not Mr. Danvers's son. Mine."

As the rest of the company gazed at him in shocked disbelief, Mr. Carrington's eyes grew unfocused, as if he were no longer seeing the very proper English drawing room, but a more exotic locale many years ago and thousands of miles away.

"Her name was Yasmina. I would have married her and damned the consequences, but it would have been death to my budding career—as my employer did not hesitate to inform me. And so, may God forgive me, I allowed myself to be persuaded to give her up. When she died in childbirth, Mr. Danvers, who was shortly to leave India, offered to take the child back to England with him. Yasmina's family accepted his offer—they were only too eager to rid their family of the stain upon its honor. The lot of a bastard half-caste is not a pleasant one; the most wretched English orphan is to be envied by comparison. Imperfect as it was, Mr. Danvers's solution appeared to be the most merciful to all involved. And yet, still I could not forget my child. When at last I retired from my position with the East India Company, I was determined to try and locate the boy. I returned to England and sought out Mr. Danvers, only to learn that the lad's foster parents were dead and the boy himself had disappeared."

Miss Grantham, sentimental soul that she was, sniffed loudly and dabbed at her eyes with a cambric handkerchief. Lady Anne heard the sound and recalled the presence of her younger daughter.

"Really, Mr. Carrington, this is hardly a fit subject for mixed company. Miss Grantham, take Susannah back to the schoolroom at once. Lady Fieldhurst, I am sure you will understand when I say that I can no longer offer you hospitality. My own carriage will convey you to the village at your convenience, from which location you may hire a post-chaise." Having dispensed with the viscountess, she fixed Pickett with a look which might have quelled a man less mindful of his duty. "As for you, Mr. Pickett, I believe you have done enough damage here. I strongly suggest that you pack your bags and leave this house at once."

As Pickett's possessions were few, it did not take him long to pack them all into a single battered valise. Having finished with this task, he started down the attic stairs, lingering for a moment on the landing nearest the schoolroom. Upon hearing muffled sobs emitting from this chamber, he tapped softly on the door and pushed it open. Miss Susannah, now clad in a light gray frock from which every scrap of lace and ribbon had been hastily removed, knelt before the fireplace. As Pickett watched, she tore a large parchment into long strips and fed them one by one into the fire.

"Miss Susannah?"

She turned at the sound of his voice, and he recognized the parchment she shredded with such care. It was the drawing she had done of him. He darted an uneasy glance down the corridor. Lady Hollingshead would doubtless expect him to depart the premises as soon as possible, but he couldn't oblige her ladyship just yet; he had unfinished business with her daughter.

"Miss Susannah, please believe that I never meant—I never thought it would end this way."

Another rip, and another strip of his face curled and blackened into oblivion. When at last she spoke, her words were the last ones Pickett would have expected. "I knew it was Papa."

He stared at her, thunderstruck. "You *knew—?*"

"The day you took me to see the gypsies wasn't the first time I'd gone into the woods to look for them. That night after dinner, while Miss Grantham was reading Mr. Danvers's book, I slipped out of the house and tried to find the gypsy camp. But the rain was still dripping off the trees, so I turned back. Emma was on the terrace with Cousin Colin, though, so I had to slip around the corner of the house before they saw me, and I almost ran straight into Papa. He was walking very quickly up the drive from the direction of the vicarage, and although he must have seen me, he walked right by like I wasn't even there. The next morning, when I heard what had happened to Mr. Danvers, I knew Papa must have—must have—"

She gave a loud sniff and wiped her nose on her sleeve, a gesture that would have brought Miss Grantham's wrath down upon her head, but one that Pickett found oddly touching. Small wonder that she had found his diary so interesting; her questions had not been inspired by morbid curiosity, but fear for the fate of a beloved parent. It was too heavy a burden for a fourteen-year-old to bear—as he had reason to know.

"When I realized you were from Bow Street," she continued, staring at the torn parchment in her lap, "I knew you would find out sooner or later. Lady Fieldhurst says you are very clever."

"I was only doing my duty, Miss Susannah. I never meant to hurt you. For what it's worth, I think I have some idea of how you feel. I lost my father when I was fourteen, too."

She threw him a skeptical, if somewhat watery, glance. "I'll bet he wasn't hanged for murder."

"No, he was transported to Botany Bay for petty thievery." Seeing her expression change to one of astonishment, he explained, "It was the only way he knew to feed his family. I know this is difficult for you, Miss Susannah, but I hope it will help you to understand that your father did what he did because he didn't want to see his family suffer for an old secret that was none of their doing."

She said nothing, but stared silently into the flames. Pickett sighed heavily, then turned toward the door. He would have left the room, but she called him back.

"John—I know it isn't proper, but may I still call you John?"

A smile touched his lips. "Please do."

"John, did Papa truly fall into the river, or did he—did he—?"

Pickett hesitated. Suicides, he knew, were buried in unconsecrated ground. For the sake of this girl, Sir Gerald should be laid to rest in the family vault, as befitted the fifth baronet Hollingshead.

"I don't know," Pickett said with perfect, if incomplete, truth. "I didn't see."

He shut the door, leaving her to grieve uninterrupted, then picked up his valise and started back down the stairs.

Pickett was almost halfway to Kendall, from which location he would board the next south-bound stage, when the rain began to fall in earnest. Trudging along the road with the heavy valise banging against his leg, he paused long enough to turn up the collar of his coat and jam his hat down more securely on his head. It didn't help much. Raindrops dripped from the brim of his hat and trickled down the back of his neck.

The *clip-clop* of horses' hooves and the jingle of harness signaled an approaching carriage. Resigning himself to splashed and muddied shoes and stockings, Pickett veered onto the shoulder of the road, giving the vehicle as wide a berth as possible. To his surprise, the carriage slowed to a crawl as it drew abreast of him and Jasper Carrington leaned forward, past the protective barrier of its hood.

"Mr. Pickett! Thank God I caught you. I wish I could offer to take you up, but as you can see, we are rather pressed for space."

Pickett looked past Mr. Carrington. Will Huggins sat beside his father on the narrow seat, clutching a bundle containing, Pickett presumed, all his worldly goods. Will's habitually hostile expression had vanished; instead, he looked more than a little dazed by his abrupt change of fortune.

Pickett could not suppress a smile. "I assure you, sir, I was never more pleased to be snubbed."

"Good man! I shan't keep you standing in the rain, but I could not let you leave without offering you some token of appreciation." He reached into the inside pocket of his coat and drew out a sealed letter, then held it out to Pickett.

"You're too kind, sir," protested Pickett, taking the letter and tucking it inside his own coat pocket.

"Nonsense! The least I could do. We'll be on our way now." Mr. Carrington patted young Will's knee. "We've a lot to catch up on, my son and I."

As the carriage lurched forward, Pickett sketched a bow (sending a fresh shower of raindrops streaming from the brim of his hat), hefted his valise, and set off down the road in their wake.

He had not traveled far when a second vehicle came bowling along the road, this one a closed carriage with a coat of arms on the side panel and a post boy perched behind the box. Recognizing the coat of arms, Pickett was all the more surprised when this vehicle, too, drew to a stop beside him and the post boy dismounted from his perch and threw open the door.

"The lady requests that you join her," he announced.

Pickett's gaze shifted from the post boy to the coach's sole occupant. "I-I couldn't," he stammered, painfully aware of his sodden state.

"Of course you can," insisted Lady Fieldhurst from within the confines of the carriage. "Unless, of course, you would rather brave the elements than endure my company."

Pickett wrestled with indecision. It was little more than a couple of miles to Kendall, by which time he could hardly be wetter than he was already; on the other hand, he was unlikely to see Lady Fieldhurst again, and certainly not in such intimate circumstances.

Never woo where you cannot hope to win . . .

It was not at all the same thing, Pickett's heart insisted, rejecting Sir Gerald's unsolicited advice out of hand. The viscountess was nothing at all like Lady Anne Hollingshead. And besides, his brain added, he was not wooing her; he had no illusions as to his eligibility as a suitor. There was, then, no reason at all why he should not accept a seat in her carriage.

His mind made up, he ducked inside the vehicle, only to recoil in dismay at the stream of water which ran off the brim of his hat to form a puddle on the carriage floor.

"Pay it no heed, Mr. Pickett." Lady Fieldhurst gestured toward to rear-facing seat. "If Lady Anne finds her carriage a bit damper than she would like, it is no more than she deserves for dismissing you in such a way."

"It wasn't raining like this when I left," Pickett reminded her, settling himself on the proffered seat and placing his valise at his feet. He did not correct the more formal manner of address. They both understood that his days of being "John" were over. "Besides, you can hardly expect her to bid me a fond farewell, after I had just single-handedly destroyed her family."

Lady Fieldhurst's expression grew solemn. "If you are thinking of Miss Susannah's outburst, pray do not refine too much upon it. She will understand better when she is a little older."

Pickett rather doubted this, but merely said, "I don't mind it, at least not much. One rarely makes friends in my line of work."

"I hope you will count me as one. Also, I suspect you have another in Mr. Carrington."

Pickett's expressive countenance lightened somewhat at the memory of father and son seated side by side beneath the hood of the rain-soaked phaeton. "Yes, that was a rather nice ending to an otherwise thoroughly bad business, wasn't it? Oh, and he gave me something."

He reached into his coat pocket and withdrew the slightly damp letter, broke the seal, and spread it open. A second, smaller rectangle of paper fluttered to the floor, and he reached down to pick it up. He took a closer look, and turned pale.

"Mr. Pickett? What is it?"

"It-it's a bank draft for one hundred pounds," he said, still staring at it in amazement.

"How very thoughtful of him," remarked Lady Fieldhurst. "What will you do with it?"

"I-I don't know," stammered Pickett. "I've never had a hundred pounds in my life."

"I should have thought Mr. Meriwether would wish to do something handsome by you, as well," continued Lady Fieldhurst. "Still, I daresay the College of Arms or some such organization must investigate the matter before he can claim his inheritance. And now that I come to think of it, I suspect Mr. Meriwether is far too tactful to appear overly eager to step into Sir Gerald's shoes."

"I don't know about that," returned Pickett with a smile. "I'll wager he'll stake his claim to Miss Hollingshead quickly enough. Can her mother do anything to stop it, do you think?"

"It would be extremely difficult for her to do so. He may even be Miss Hollingshead's legal guardian, now that her father is dead. And that is another thing that puzzles me," she continued, regarding him with a measuring look. "I don't understand how you could allow Sir Gerald to fall into the river like that. Such carelessness seems unlike you."

Pickett gazed fixedly out the window. "I expect Mr. Colquhoun will wonder about that, too."

"Confess, Mr. Pickett! You allowed Sir Gerald to cheat the hangman by taking his own life. But *why*, pray tell?"

Pickett had asked himself that same question many times already throughout the course of the morning and suspected it would haunt him for some time to come. He knew there were Runners past and present with a well-deserved reputation for corruption, and he could not quite shake the nagging conviction that he had just joined their ranks. After all, he had told Miss Susannah that it was not his place to dispense justice, but in the end he had done exactly that. And yet, if he had it to do over again, he very much feared he would do the same thing.

Seeing that her ladyship still awaited his answer, Pickett merely shrugged. "I discovered we had something in common."

She waited for him to elaborate, but he said no more on the subject, and soon the carriage lurched to a stop in the bustling courtyard of the posting-house. Pickett had almost an hour to wait for the next south-bound stagecoach; by contrast, when the viscountess requested the hire of a private post-chaise and a team of horses, a suitable vehicle was brought out almost at once—far too promptly, at any rate, for Pickett's liking. Nevertheless, he took a certain proprietary pleasure in hefting her ladyship's considerable baggage and seeing it stored securely in the boot.

"If you should happen to think of it," Pickett said, as the driver opened the carriage door and let down the step, "will you thank Thomas for the use of his livery and tell him I will return it as soon as I reach London?"

Lady Fieldhurst eschewed the driver's proffered assistance, and offered her hand to Pickett instead. "Certainly. It does seem strange to be going back to London. And to think Emily Dunnington assured me that I should be shockingly bored within a week! It will be good to be back in my own home and surrounded by my own servants. I must confess, though, that I shall rather miss John Footman."

"I can't imagine why." Pickett took her ladyship's hand and steadied her as she mounted the step. "The fellow was incompetent."

"I wouldn't say that," protested Lady Fieldhurst. "I found him rather adept—at some things."

She gave him a mischievous smile, then disappeared into the dark interior of the chaise before Pickett could ask her to elaborate. Then the driver shut the door and mounted the box, and in another moment the carriage was clattering out of the courtyard and into the High Street.

She was referring to his solving the mystery of Mr. Danvers's murder, Pickett told himself firmly. She had to be. She could hardly be thinking of his adroitness at the breakfast table. Unless . . . was it possible that she was remembering that midnight kiss in the library? No, of course not. It was absurd to even imagine such a thing. And yet . . .

Unmindful of the rain, Pickett stood there in the courtyard for a long moment, a singularly foolish smile playing about his mouth as he watched the post-chaise rattle down the High Street and southward toward London.

ABOUT THE AUTHOR

Sheri Cobb South is the award-winning author of five regency novels, including *The Weaver Takes a Wife, Miss Darby's Duenna,* and *Of Paupers and Peers.* She has also written a number of teen romances for Bantam's long-running Sweet Dreams series, and her short fiction has appeared in national magazines such as *Woman's World, Teen,* and *Campus Life.* She made her mystery debut in 2006 with the publication of *In Milady's Chamber,* which introduced Bow Street Runner John Pickett. Sheri lives in Mobile, Alabama, with her family and loves to hear from readers. She may be contacted at Cobbsouth@aol.com.